a very

keatyn christmas

THE

keatyn

CHRONICLES

a very keatyn christmas

JILLIAN DODD

Published by Swoonworthy Books, an imprint of
Jillian Dodd, Inc.
www.jilliandodd.net

ISBN: 978-1-953071-53-8

Books by Jillian Dodd

London Prep
The Exchange
The Boys' Club
The Kiss
The Key
The Party

The Keatyn Chronicles®
Stalk Me
Kiss Me
Date Me
Love Me
Adore Me
Hate Me
Get Me
Fame
Power
Money
Sex
Love
Keatyn Unscripted
Aiden

That Boy
That Boy
That Wedding

That Baby
That Love
That Ring
That Summer
That Promise

Kitty Valentine
Kitty Valentine dates a Billionaire
Kitty Valentine dates a Doctor
Kitty Valentine dates a Rockstar
Kitty Valentine dates a Fireman
Kitty Valentine dates an Actor
Kitty Valentine dates the Best Man
Kitty Valentine dates a Cowboy
Kitty Valentine dates a Hockey Player
Kitty Valentine dates Santa

Crawford Brothers
Vegas Love
Broken Love
Fake Love

Spy Girl®
The Prince
The Eagle
The Society
The Valiant
The Dauntless
The Phoenix
The Echelon

Girl off the Grid

List of characters, their children's names and current ages.

Aiden & Keatyn Arrington

—Asher **Monroe** (15)

—Aubrey **Lane** (15)

—**Aspen** Stevens (15)

—Ashton **Steele** (10)

—**Arden** Duncan (8)

Dawson & Vanessa Johnson

—Ava (26)

—Harlow (23)

—Branson (15)

Riley & Ariela Johnson

—Mason (14)

—Emerson (13)

—Hadley (1 1/2)

Camden & Annie Johnson

—Parker (21)

—Sutton (20)

—Callan (19)

—**Beck**ham (16)

Damian & Peyton Moran

—Jagger (21)

—Jett (19)

—Cash (16)

Tommy Stevens & Abby Johnston

—Keatyn Douglas (44)

—Avery (33)

—Emery (33)

—Ivery (33)

—Gracelyn (31)

—Lincoln (27)

Brady Wright & Gracie Stevens

—Waverly (14)

Dallas & RiAnne McMahon

—Fallon (27)

—Carder (24)

—Finley (22)

—Teagan (19)

—Farryn (16)

December 23rd

THE SHOOTING STAR.
AUBREY LANE

"LANE, CAN I help you braid Sparky's mane?" my little sister, Arden, asks me. "And do you think we can put ribbons in it too?"

"Of course, Arden," I tell her as I continue to brush my horse. "Why don't you go in the tack room and get the red and green velvet?"

"I already tried to," she says with a little huff. "It's up too high for me to reach."

I take a moment to look and see what's going on around me. My brothers, Monroe and Aspen, are carefully touching up the paint on a horse-drawn carriage made to look like Santa's sleigh. My great-grandpa Douglas, who we call Doogie, is helping my youngest brother, Steele, organize all the bridles, harnesses, and reins.

I love the rhythmic motion of brushing my horse. It's almost therapeutic. But clearly, I was totally lost in thought. Tomorrow kicks off a full week of holiday

1

celebrations with family and friends. And I should be focused on that, but I'm not because something is bothering me.

Or I should say, someone.

I pick up my little sister and sit her up on my horse's back. Sparky is really gentle and loves being groomed.

"I'll go get all the pretty ribbons for you," I tell her.

"Grab the bell harnesses while you're in there," Doogie says. "We need to get them fitted, so they're ready to go for the parade."

I get the harnesses and take them back out, jingling all the way, causing Monroe to start singing "Jingle Bells." And pretty soon, we're all singing it together.

When I get the ribbons over to Sparky's stall, Arden tells me, "Sparky wants to go outside for a ride."

I smile at her. "Sparky wants to or *you* want to?"

"Both!" she yells. "Then Sparky wants us to make her all pretty. Like a Christmassy rainbow pony."

A few moments later, I'm leading the horse around the corral while Arden sits on her back and talks to her. "Sparky, did you know that Santa is going to bring me a pony for Christmas this year, so you're going to have a new pony friend?"

I'm not really paying that much attention to her chatter, but then she shouts, "Look, Lane! A shooting star! We have to make a wish!"

I glance up and see the star, its long tail blazing

behind it.

"I wish for a pony!" Arden screams.

And I make my own wish.

Which brings me back to who I was thinking about earlier—Branson Johnson. He has been my best friend since kindergarten. My brothers and I are close—I mean, we are triplets after all—but I've always been the one to want to strike out on my own, choosing Branson as my best friend when Monroe and Aspen would only play with each other.

We all had big plans to go to Eastbrooke Academy together our freshman year. His parents let him go. Ours didn't, deciding at the last minute that they wanted us to wait until we were juniors.

Which means we won't be back together full-time until next fall.

And it sucks.

Because my parents are alums, our family goes there for the homecoming festivities, so I usually get to be his date for the dance. Last year, I got to fly out for his winter formal, but this year, my dad was out of the country, and Mom was freaking out about finishing the film she was working on and said she just couldn't deal with it.

I really think she had no idea how crushed I was. Probably because of my possible *crush*—on Branson. I'd had grand visions for the dance. Me in a gorgeous dress, him finally realizing we should be more than just friends, and a night that would've ended with a kiss.

My *first* kiss.

While Branson said he understood, the dance was on the eighteenth, and he hasn't texted me once since then. Granted, I know he's probably really busy. The day after the dance, he took the train to New York City to meet his parents for a few days of shopping before traveling to their family's big celebration in the Hamptons.

So, when I saw the shooting star, I couldn't help it. I wished that Branson would kiss me before the end of this year.

Which means it'd better work fast because there are only, like, seven days left.

THOSE KINDS OF FRIENDSHIPS.
KEATYN

AIDEN AND I get home at the exact same time.

And we're both late.

"Wow, the winery's holiday party must have been quite the bash this year," I tease, greeting him with a quick kiss. "Sorry I couldn't be there."

"The party was over fast. We closed down at four. I handed out year-end bonus checks and surprised them all by saying that we were closing until January 6 and to go enjoy themselves until then."

"You're closing for that long?"

"Yep. I've been planning it for a while, so we didn't book any tastings or weddings. But after surviving mudslides and fires and all the other chaos in the world, we all need a nice, long break. I thought I told you about it."

"You might have. Sorry, I've been a little distracted, trying to finish this movie."

He gives me a deeper kiss, one that tastes of whiskey, not wine.

"Just what have you been up to since then?"

He grabs me around the waist, dips me back, and goes, "Ho, ho, ho," before planting another kiss on my lips.

"Oh gosh, did you lose the drink-off for Santa this year?"

"Yep," he says in mock sorrow.

The drink-off for Santa is something that all the men who live on what is now a big tract of adjoining properties we lovingly call The Enclave do, playing drinking games to see who has the honor of being Santa at our annual holiday party.

"Logan played even though he and Maggie are leaving on their vacation tomorrow and won't be here. He was supposedly filling in for Knox, who joined us late since he was still filming with you—which I thought was unfair, but whatever—and Riley and Dawson played via video chat from the Hamptons." He kisses my neck. "I take it you stayed to look at the dailies?"

"I did. And they were good. It's officially a wrap," I tell him happily.

"Perfect timing," he says with a smirk. "You know, I bet you're really tired. I should probably get you to bed. And we should hurry before the kids get home."

"Where are they? I figured they were probably already asleep."

"They're working on a project," he says, leading me toward our room. "Don't worry. Grandpa is supervising. And there's a big bathtub calling our name."

"Sounds like the perfect way to kick off *our* holiday."

Of course, we don't make it to the bath right away. That comes after he picks me up and tosses me on the bed and proceeds to remind me why I married him.

Okay. Maybe I didn't marry him *just* for sex, but he still makes my heart flutter and takes my breath away almost as much as our very first time.

I'M LEANING BACK against his chest in the tub while he cups warm water and pours it down the front of me.

"You were talking about the chaos in the world," I say dreamily. "You know, you're still my control in it all."

He leans down and kisses my neck. "Hard to believe we've been married for sixteen years already. Seems like yesterday, we were just a couple of kids at school."

"I know. And our kids are growing up way too fast. I can't believe they'll be going to Eastbrooke next fall."

"They should have gone their freshman year," he counters.

"I couldn't do it, Aiden. They are so well-traveled and articulate and smart, but they've been really sheltered here. I was afraid to send them too soon. Not to mention the fact that I will miss them terribly."

"The boys didn't seem to mind, but Lane was upset about it."

"That's because she didn't want to be away from Branson," I tell him.

"He *has* been her best friend for most of her life. Well, since Dawson and Vanessa moved out here full-time."

I let out another sigh. "I really hope they enjoy Eastbrooke as much as we did. That they make those kinds of friendships."

"I will admit that when I followed my sister to some East Coast boarding school," he says, "I never imagined I would meet the love of my life, realize my dream of owning a vineyard, and work and live in close proximity to so many of my friends. All because of Eastbrooke."

"It's funny really. Before I got sent there, I wanted my two sets of friends to come together. And eventually, they did. Dawson married Vanessa, Dallas married RiAnne, Knox and Katie met at our wedding, and they all became close with Maggie and Logan and Riley and Ariela."

"And don't forget our Thanksgiving in St. Croix, where my sister met Damian."

"Crazy, right?" I say, because it really is. I also know we are really fortunate.

"And now, all our kids are friends too. And with

the changes Braxton has made at Eastbrooke—"

"I still can't believe that he is now the school's dean," I say with a laugh. "Can you? I loved him from the moment I met him back when he was a cocky little eighth grader—even with that potty mouth of his. He just cracked me up. Still does really."

"Well, he certainly knows the kids' tricks since he's probably done it all before."

"And then some." I continue to laugh.

"You know Lane will do well. She loved being in Paris by herself this summer, working at The Arrington there. She told me she wants to run that company someday."

"First off, she wasn't by herself. In Paris. At fifteen," I counter.

"You know what I mean. She wasn't with us. And she probably *will* run it someday. She wants to intern in London next summer."

The thought of not seeing my kids most every day makes me sad, but I know that it's time.

We hear commotion coming from the kitchen.

"I guess bath time is over," Aiden says.

"We could pretend to be asleep," I offer, knowing that won't happen.

WE GET OUT of the tub, put on robes, and head in the direction of the noise. And I can't help but smile, seeing all my children around the kitchen island, making late-night nachos—one of their favorite snacks.

It's amazing how all five look related, but each

takes after Aiden and me in different ways.

The triplets—Asher Monroe, Aubrey Lane, and Aspen Stevens—have such varied personalities. Monroe is the tallest of the group, already six foot tall. He's an Aiden mini-me, except for his striking blue-purple eyes, which were passed from my dad to me. His light-brown hair is either shagging in his eyes or shoved straight back in almost a pompadour style. He loves meeting people and trying to figure out what makes them tick. He's very laid-back, and he plays guitar, writes music and poetry, and appears perpetually bored even though he's not. His mind is always going, even when you don't realize it, and he remembers everything everyone says. Right now, he's sitting on a barstool, playing Christmas songs on his guitar amid the chaos around him.

Aspen, even though he is the youngest of the trio, is the drill sergeant of the family and is always trying to tell all of us—including me and Aiden—what to do. He's currently assigning tasks to everyone to get the nachos made. Although he must have preplanned to make them tonight since it's obvious our long-time chef, Marvel, made sure all the fixings were prepped.

And while all of our kids are athletic—of course, Aiden had them playing soccer from the time they could walk—Aspen is the most driven. In fact, I'd say he thrives on competition. And while Monroe's hair is usually all over the place, Aspen's is always perfectly styled.

"Mommy! Daddy!" is yelled out when Arden—our youngest daughter, who will be turning eight in a few days—spots us. "You'll never guess what we've been doing!"

She runs over to me, and I pick her right up. She says she's getting too old for it, but tonight, she jumps happily into my arms. I can tell by her eyes that she's sleepy.

"What have you been doing, Arden?" Aiden asks her, giving her a kiss on the top of her head.

"We decorated the ponies for Christmas!"

"Did you mistake them for trees?" Aiden teases.

"No, Daddy. We're going to have a sleigh ride. And a Christmas parade! And Doogie said the ponies had to look beautiful for it."

We actually are having a Christmas parade. Her birthday is the twenty-sixth and also falls on the same day as our annual holiday party this year, so we're going all out.

Our youngest son, Ashton Steele, who is ten, rushes over to get in on the action, jumping into Aiden's arms and confirming, "It's true. We brushed them and put ribbons in their manes, and on Arden's birthday, Doogie is going to put bells on them!"

"All for my very own birthday!" Arden yells.

Obviously, the cat's out of the bag on that one.

"Hey, you two," Monroe scolds, "don't you have some chips to spread on the pan?"

The kids jump out of our arms and start chanting, "Nachos, nachos!"

"I don't think I ever got a Christmas parade for my birthday," Aubrey Lane says, rolling her eyes. "And I'm the one in the family who likes horses the most."

"I'm just really, really special," Arden tells her very seriously. "Because my birthday is at Christmas, and sometimes, people with Christmas birthdays don't like it that everyone gets to open presents on their birthday."

To which Lane can't help but smile. And she should. She's just as precocious.

She lifts her little sister up and sets her on the counter. "Why don't you spread the chips out while I put on the taco meat?" She whispers in her ear, "And I bet Santa might leave you something extra under the tree."

Watching their interaction warms my heart. All our kids are gathered in the kitchen. There's garland hanging over the island and twinkle lights in the windows. The tree was decorated last week and sits adjacent to the fireplace.

I lean my head against Aiden's and sigh contentedly. "I love you," I tell him. "And the life we've created."

"Our kids are pretty cool, don't you think?"

"Ifly you all," I whisper.

"Oh my gosh," Lane says to me, "we can hear you. And thankfully, the little kids don't know what that means."

I bite my tongue. I adore my daughter, but she knows how to push my buttons—just like I did with my mother, I suppose. We've never allowed them to watch the movies about our lives, but there's a popular song now with the same term, so they finally understand what we've been saying to each other all these years.

"What does what mean?" Steele asks. He's busy tossing cheese all over the chips.

"It means the nachos are almost ready to go in the oven!" Aspen tells him, thankfully changing the subject.

"I think I'm going to dye my hair," Lane says randomly. "What do you think, Arden? Would I look pretty if my hair was browner?"

"I think you're bea-u-tiful just the way you are. You have hair like Sparky. Long and pretty."

"Sparky's hair is brown," Lane tells her sister and then turns to us. "Do you think Marnie would be willing to come over sometime soon to dye my hair?"

"I think she's probably going to be spending time with her family," Aiden tells her, referring to the hairstylist who does hair for all the weddings we have at the vineyard.

Arden interjects, "No dyeing your hair. I like that our hair matches. Just like Mommy's. I wanna be like Mommy when I grow up. Only I'm going to ride horses in my movies."

Monroe stops strumming and says, "Oh, really?"

I can tell that he's actually really interested. Especially when you would have assumed he wasn't even listening.

"Yes. Or I am going to be an e-quest-er-an."

"You mean, an equestrian?" Aiden offers.

"Yes. A person who rides horses in shows and makes them dance. I love that. Remember how they danced on TV during the Olympics?"

"I do remember," Monroe says to her. "It's called dressage, and it's known as the ballet of horseback riding. But do you remember what happened when Lane tried to teach Sparky?"

"Sparky was not happy," Arden says.

There's a bark at the back door, and I see my grandpa through the glass.

"Doogie and Lucky are here!" Steele says, jumping off the counter and flinging open the door.

The dog barrels into the room, covering Steele's face with kisses like they have been separated for days instead of a few minutes.

"Doogie!" Arden says, holding her hands out toward him. "I told everyone about how you helped us decorate the horses."

"I hear there's going to be a Christmas *and* a birthday parade," I say, smiling.

"Sure is," he says to me before turning to Aiden. "Got anything to warm this old man's bones?"

"You know I do." Aiden moves toward the bar, pours two glasses of whiskey, and leads Grandpa over to the chairs in front of the fire.

I let out a sad sigh. Grandma Douglas passed away this spring, and it's going to be our first Christmas without her. And even though I was crazy busy with work, I was bound and determined to get the movie done so that I could continue all our holiday traditions in her honor. Grandpa Douglas is getting older, as we all are, but he's still in really great shape and just as ornery as ever. But her passing has taken a toll on him.

He glances at the kids in the kitchen and over to

the chair where Aiden takes a seat, which was her spot when she was here, and looks sad for a moment. But when the kids get the nachos out of the oven, spread everything on the big coffee table, and gather on the floor around it, he smiles.

"One of you hoodlums, fix your Doogie a plate, will you? I'm the one who made sure all the horses were put up."

"I'll do it!" Arden screeches, grabbing a plate and putting a messy pile of nachos on it and then presenting it to him along with a paper towel.

"Thank you, Arden," he says, patting her on the head. "You're already a good cook. Just like your grandma."

"I miss Grammy," Arden says.

"We all do," the kids say in unison.

"You know she's here with us in spirit," Grandpa says. "And she wouldn't want none of us crying about her not being here when we're supposed to be kicking off the holidays. It was her favorite time of the year."

Arden makes up her own plate and then goes and sits at Grandpa's feet along with Lucky—the third—who would love a plate of his own and knows she's an easy target.

"Play us another Christmas song, Monroe," Arden orders.

"After I get my nachos," he fires back in a sing-song voice.

I watch as Lane piles nachos on a couple plates, passing them out to her brothers. Of course, we all think our children are amazing, but I love that she still has no idea just how beautiful she is. She's carefree, not into clothes and makeup like I was at her age. Loves sports, riding horses, and just hanging out.

Aiden and I made the decision years ago to set up a school here on our property. After my experience with a stalker and my high-profile career, I really felt the need to protect them. And although they have traveled a lot with us, we've done a really good job of keeping them out of the spotlight. None of them are allowed social media accounts, and I never post photos of them on mine. There's plenty of time for that when they are older.

Lane has always sort of tried to mother her broth-ers—maybe more like tried to *smother* them half the time. Aspen resists, but she and Monroe tend to never fight because he's just so easygoing. Of all the kids, she favors the Arrington side and looks more like Aiden's sister, Peyton, than me—the three of them share the same set of striking green eyes. When I was her age, I had no idea what I wanted to do or be, but she seems to already have her life figured out. Eastbrooke. Cambridge. London School of Economics for an advanced business degree. Then taking over The Arrington chain, which now has locations in over twenty major cities around the world.

"Mom, Dad, do you guys want any?" Lane asks, interrupting my thoughts.

"Actually, I'd love some," I say, suddenly realizing it's been a while since I've eaten.

"Add a few extra for me," Aiden tells her. "We'll share."

Just as she hands us our plate, her phone buzzes. She reads it with a smile then quickly throws nachos on a plate and says, "I'm going to take these up to my room and eat while I, uh, read. Night, everyone!"

But I know exactly why she wants to go to her room.

Because there's only one person who makes her smile like that.

THE THOUGHT OF HIM.
AUBREY LANE

I MAYBE JUMP a little when Branson Johnson's name pops up on my phone.

> **Branson:** It sucked not having you at winter formal with me this year. I still don't understand why you couldn't have just brought the plane, like usual.

And since we haven't talked in days, I tell everyone good night and take my nachos up to my room before I reply.

Because I desperately need to know something.

> **Me:** Did you end up taking a date?

I wait for what feels like ten hours. The little dots on the screen taunting me as he types.

The dots disappear—like he doesn't know what to say.

And my heart maybe breaks just a little.

The dots come back.

And I *finally* get his response.

Branson: *No.*

I let out a huge sigh of relief. And I don't know why. It's not like we are boyfriend and girlfriend or anything. We literally are just friends. But he's my best friend, and the thought of him kissing someone else sort of makes my stomach churn.

> **Me:** *I'm going to ask my dad if he will let me come to Eastbrooke in January instead of waiting until next fall. That's soooo far away.*
> **Branson:** *I miss you.*
> **Me:** *I miss you too.*
> **Branson:** *But I will see you in three days for the party, and then we'll have fun, going skiing.*
> **Me:** *We always do! And since your uncle Riley is the lucky chaperone this year...*
> **Branson:** *We can do whatever we want.*
> **Me:** *Exactly. So, what do we want to do?*
> **Branson:** *I want to sleep with you, for starters.*

Wait. What?

I mean, I want to be more than friends, but . . . I'm not at all ready for that.

> **Me:** *Uh...*

His response is almost immediate, like we were typing at the same time.

> **Branson:** *I mean, like, be in the bed with you. Hang out, just the two of us. I didn't mean, like, sex.*

And although I'm relieved by that, I'm also sort of disappointed. *Does it mean he's not attracted to me in that way?*

Me: *Oh.*

Just as I send the text, I'm startled by the phone vibrating in my hand.

His name pops up on the screen, and when I answer, he says, "Hey, Laney."

"Hey, Brannie."

"I think what I was trying to say wasn't coming across correctly over text."

"I like it better when you call me anyway. You know that," I say happily.

It's good to hear his voice. I can almost pretend he's here, in my room, spinning around on my fluffy vanity chair.

"I do. But I'm in the Hamptons with all my cousins and the whole family. No privacy."

"Do you need privacy to talk to me?" *What is he going to say?*

"No, it's just that they'll all tease me about you being my girlfriend."

"And you'll say what you always do—that we're just friends and my being a girl has nothing to do with it."

Except it kinda maybe does.

"Because we're getting older, I suppose," he offers. "And you've been my date to all my dances, so they kind of think we're a thing."

"And what do you think?" I dare to ask.

He sucks in a breath. And I'm thinking I'm glad he didn't ask me this question because I don't know what the answer would be.

Or maybe it's that I'm afraid to know.

"What do you think?" he asks.

"I asked you first," I fire back, trying to make my voice sound light and teasing.

"Well, we've never kissed, so I would say that clearly puts us in the friends category."

"Yes, it does. Definitely," I reply, feeling disappointed.

We've never really talked about this, but I thought . . . maybe. Like, someday. *I mean, why does he keep asking me to go to his dances?*

"But . . ."

"But what?" I say breathlessly, falling back dramatically on my bed in anticipation.

"I think I'd like that to change, Laneybug."

"Like, *date* or something?"

"Yeah. Maybe. If you are open to it."

My heart soars, but I try to play it cool. "I think I am, actually." *OMG!! Yay!! Did my wish work?*

"Good," he says, his voice low and dreamy. I swear, I could listen to him talk all day. "You know, if we kiss on New Year's Eve, that'll make you mine for the year."

"It will?"

"I'm pretty sure, yeah," he says in a serious tone. "Which means when you come to Eastbrooke, whether it's this winter or next fall, we could be—well, we could hang out a lot. Since we'd be together again, finally."

"I can't wait for that."

I hear his name being called out in the background.

"Sorry, I gotta go. Grandma is making us play holiday charades."

I can't help but laugh. "You know, with your cousins, that is going to end badly."

"Why do you say that?"

"Because they all have dirty minds. What if one of them gets the song 'Santa Claus Is *Coming* to Town,' or there's something like, *Jingle my bells*."

"Laney! I never knew you had such a dirty mind. You might have just ruined Christmas for me with those visuals."

"Really?" I ask, feeling bad. Clearly, I have hung out with all the Johnson boys and my brothers so much that they have rubbed off on me.

He laughs. "I'm just teasing. Maybe the game will be more interesting than I thought." He lowers his voice to a whisper. "I like that you have a dirty mind."

"It's you boys' fault," I tease. "Bye, Branson."

"Bye, Laney."

I hang up with a contented sigh and start counting down the minutes until he'll be back home. Because things just got interesting.

December 24th

A DISASTER TOGETHER.
KEATYN

I WAKE UP early, both excited and nervous for the day. Today, we'll bake and decorate cookies together, snack and drink hot cocoa and spiced cider, play Christmas music, and enjoy spending time with each other.

And my family will arrive at some point.

At least, some of them will. I've always had a close relationship with my mom and Tommy, but there's been a lot of drama in their lives with my half sisters, and as with family drama, people tend to take sides. I try to be Switzerland, but that doesn't always work either.

I pull myself out of bed and get ready for the day, dressing in a festive sweater, velvet leggings, and fluffy slippers. We'll dress up more tonight for dinner, but today is all about comfort.

Aiden rolls toward me as I come out of the bathroom. "You're up early."

"I am."

"Do you know who's coming this year?"

"Not so far. As usual, they were all invited, and we'll welcome whoever shows up with open arms."

He knows it all bothers me, so he sweetly says, "Why don't I get up and make us a good breakfast?"

I plop down on the bed next to him and give him a kiss. "As in cinnamon waffles with pecan caramel sauce and spicy fried potatoes?"

"Is there any other kind of *good* around here?" he teases.

"Well, the kids do like chocolate chip and blueberry waffles too."

He slides his hand down my arm and says in a low, sexy voice, "What do *you* want?"

"You, of course. Always. But . . . right now . . ."

"Waffles for the win?"

"Basically, yes. Come on. Get up. It's going to be a good day." At least, that's what I keep telling myself.

"Have you heard if Ivery will be able to make it?"

I shake my head, feeling sad and a bit helpless about the situation. "No, she's the only one I know for sure won't be here. She'll be staying in rehab for at least a few more weeks. But I'm proud of her for making the decision. She seems to be really trying this time. And I think she and Evan broke up for good."

"He wasn't exactly supportive," Aiden says. "I mean, who takes someone fresh out of a stint in rehab to Vegas to celebrate?"

"They were a disaster together," I agree.

"What about Gracie?"

"You know how that usually goes. She says she is coming, but then there's always some last-minute excuse. I'm not holding my breath."

"She and your mom haven't really gotten along since—"

"Since she got pregnant and married Brooklyn's nephew, Brady, when they were so young."

"They've been together for almost fifteen years. You'd think the family would all be over it by now," Aiden says.

"It's hard though, you know. Gracie was so excited to go to Eastbrooke. She was having so much fun there, finally just being a teen. She had told us she was done with Brady and was dating that Baylor Hawthorne guy. Remember him?"

Aiden nods.

"Then we find out she's pregnant with Brady's baby. It was all such a shock."

"Still," Aiden says. "Even though they were young, she and Brady have done well. Waverly is a great kid."

"Hard to believe Gracie was Lane's age when she got pregnant. And I know the kids want to go to Eastbrooke, and I know we promised that they could when they were juniors, but what if that happens to one of them?"

"Hopefully, we've taught them two things about sex. That it's better to wait until they are older, and if they don't, to use protection. And no matter what happens, they know we'll fully and completely support them," Aiden says. "Just like we did with Gracie. She and Waverly lived with us for quite a while."

"Until she turned eighteen and got married."

"And then had a very successful reality TV show."

"*Raising Waverly* was a big hit, for sure. I can't believe Gracie talked me into doing that. I felt like it was . . . I don't know, so intrusive and almost promoting teen pregnancy, which I struggled with. And it pissed my mom and Tommy off in the process."

"You never know what life is going to throw at you, Boots. You make the best of it. Which Gracie did. For whatever it's worth, I'm proud of her. And she has always known that you are too."

"She's always been special to me. I'm going to call her this morning. Beg her not to cancel."

"Good luck," he says, giving me another kiss and then moving off the bed and into our closet to get dressed.

WHILE AIDEN IS preparing breakfast, I make myself a cup of tea and call my little sister. I know it's early, but if she's going to be up here in time, she has to be getting ready to leave.

She answers with, "Hey," and I can already hear it in her voice.

"Well, what's the verdict, Gracie?"

"I've decided to go visit Ivery today. I got it approved with the staff there, so I'm going to have to miss this year. We don't want her to be alone on a holiday."

"And if she wasn't in rehab?"

"Don't, Keatyn, okay?"

"Mom and Tommy are only going to be here today, and then they're leaving for Florida to spend Christmas Day with Grandma Stevens."

"We're doing Christmas Day with Brady's family."

"New Year's Eve then?"

"Not this year. I would. Seriously, I would. But Waverly has a party to go to that is—well, you remember how it was—the most important event ever in her life."

I let out a laugh. "I do remember those days."

"Yeah, me too," she says, sounding a little sad. She had choices, but for her, the only option was to have the baby and then to raise Waverly herself, no matter how young she was.

"We need to get together after the holidays then. It's been too long. Could we set a date, like, now? It could be your Christmas present to me."

"I already sent your presents," she says.

"Still."

"I'm throwing Brady a surprise birthday party in January. Would you all like to come?"

"We'd love to, Gracie. Thank you, and Merry Christmas!"

"Merry Christmas," she replies. "And thanks for understanding. I know you want the family all together, but—"

"I love you regardless. Always," I tell her.

"And for that, I'm grateful," she says before saying good-bye.

"I TAKE IT, that's a no?" Aiden asks, startling me.

I was sort of lost in thought, trying to figure out how I could fix the situation.

"Yeah, but we're invited to Brady's birthday party in January, so we'll see them then. And she said she's going to visit Ivery—hard to argue with that."

"There's only so much you can control," Aiden says simply. "Now, come over here and taste the caramel sauce."

I nod at him, get up, and let go of all of it. I'll enjoy spending time with whoever in the family decides to show up today. Then it will be Christmas Day with just our immediate family and then Christmas with our friends along with Arden's birthday party on the twenty-sixth.

"I SMELL BACON!" Steele says, running down the stairs toward the kitchen.

He is such a little cutie, and I love his sweet personality.

"It's not quite done yet," Aiden tells him. "You want to go wake up your brothers and sisters?"

"I'll wake up Arden but no one else. Teens like to sleep in late. And it's too bad. Sometimes, they miss all the good stuff," he replies.

I watch as Monroe sneaks up behind him, picks him up, and throws him over his shoulder playfully. "Maybe you're missing all the good stuff by going to sleep early," he suggests as he wanders into the family room and drops his brother down on one of the couches before tickling him.

"I smell bacon," Aspen says, rolling down a few moments later.

This causes Steele to laugh. "See, I don't even need to wake them up. The smell of bacon is doing it for me."

"What time is everyone going to be here?" Aspen asks.

"I'm not sure. They were given our schedule and were told to come whenever they wanted to. So, cookie baking and decorating commences in T-minus seventy minutes. Or as soon as Dad gets the kitchen cleaned up."

"Hey, I'm cooking," Aiden argues. "Someone else gets to do the dishes."

"Monroe," I say, "will you go wake up your sisters?"

"No need," Lane says, coming down the stairs with Arden in tow.

"Well, merry Christmas Eve!" I say happily because they are really all that matters.

ONCE WE'RE ALL seated with plates full of food, Aiden looks at me and smiles. "Boots, I think you should do a toast to kick off the holiday."

And I know in this moment the exact one I want to use. One from a long time ago, from when Aiden and I were in St. Croix for Thanksgiving—the toast Damian's dad always used.

I raise my orange juice up in the air. "It's times like these that we stop to reflect on our lives. On the things we have to be thankful for. Thornton Wilder once wrote, *We can only be said to be alive in those moments when our hearts are conscious of our treasures.* In other words, look at the people gathered around you, the food sitting before you, and the beauty that surrounds you. Merry Christmas!"

We all clink our juice glasses together, mine landing last on Aiden's.

He mouths to me, *It will all be okay*, and because

he said it, I know it is true.

He's always had some sort of godly power over me, clearly. Of course, he's moving his lips right now, his mouth mesmerizing me.

"Get a room," Lane says in a sort of teasing way but still rolls her eyes.

"Don't say that to us," I chastise.

"It's just kind of gross when you look at each other, all lovey-dovey."

"Would you prefer we hated each other, fought all the time, and then got a divorce?" Aiden counters, taking my side while appealing to her logical nature.

She narrows her eyes, thinking through this possibility. She's so not like me. I always tried to be respectful to my mom and Tommy, but I would have fired back some smart-ass comment in this situation.

Finally, she tilts her head and says, "No, that wouldn't be good."

"I wanna marry someone just like Daddy," Arden says.

Of course, she's still young enough to think her parents are the best.

GRANDPA DOUGLAS JOINS us as we're just finishing up, managing to snag a couple waffles.

"Are you ready to make cookies, Doogie?" Steele asks him.

"I'm ready to *eat* cookies," he replies.

"Oh, come on. You have to decorate at least one!" Arden says, knowing for the most part that she has my big, tough grandfather wrapped around her little finger.

"Fine," he agrees.

Just as we're ready to get started, Aiden's parents arrive. The kids are thrilled to see them. They have a guesthouse here for when they visit but have taken to condo life in Palm Springs. They have made so many friends there and are so busy that, sometimes, it's hard to drag them away.

And of course, they are right on time.

One of the things I greatly appreciate about them.

THREE AND A half hours and dozens of our favorite cookies baked and decorated later, we hear a car in the driveway.

"They're here! They're here!" Arden shouts.

We all go to the door to greet my mother, Tommy, and my youngest half-sibling, Lincoln. He's extremely handsome, and he lives in LA with his husband and interior design business partner, Nate, and their two-and-a-half-year-old twin boys. The boys are dressed in adorable matching Gucci plaid pants and holiday sweaters that were probably custom-made for the occasion. Soon, they will be covered in frosting.

Avery and her husband of six months, David, arrive some thirty minutes later. Following them are Emery, whose music career is still thriving, and Kenny, her drummer boyfriend of six months.

After greetings and lots of hugs and kisses, we offer everyone cookies and cider.

I do notice that David pulls Aiden aside and speaks to him in private. Not that surprising because David owns numerous restaurants that want to carry the Asher Vineyards brand. So far, Aiden hasn't done a deal with him. Mostly because the higher-priced wines we produce are purchased by our club members and any extras are then allotted to The Arrington chain and our restaurant clients—from oldest to newest. David's restaurants are nice and have great food, but it's a large chain, and they want to buy out every boutique wine we make. And Aiden won't do that to the customers who have been with us since when we were just getting started. Aiden's offered him our Moon Wish line. It raises money for charitable causes, is sold in mass, and the grapes are sourced from other growers. Which means production could be ramped up to fulfill his needs, but David wants the premier labels. And even goes as far as suggesting he just might buy us out.

Which, in my opinion, is a little rude. And impossible since we'd never sell.

Let's just say that Aiden isn't a fan of his and is probably ready for him to leave.

Grandpa, of course, steps in the middle of the conversation, cuffs David on the shoulder, and then says, "It's Christmas. No business talk today."

My kids love playing with their twin cousins. Watching them toddle around. Feeding them cookies. Letting them pet Lucky.

We're sort of in that awkward space before dinner, and I know I should probably get a game out to help us pass the time.

But Aiden has a different idea. "Who's ready for a drink?" he asks, which gets a lively response from all, including my own children, who are dying to try the new flavored root beers we got for the occasion.

CHEESY LOVE STORIES.
AUBREY LANE

THINGS ARE ALWAYS crazy when my mom's family is here. They are all awesome but live such separate lives.

I felt a little bad I told my parents to get a room at breakfast. Well, I felt bad after I thought about what my dad had said. Because he was right.

While Mimi and Grampy are pretty normal grandparents—as far as grandparents who are superstar actors go—they don't spend all that much time with us. I think maybe it's because they have their hands full with my aunts.

Avery runs a PR firm, and while I know she is successful, she likes to constantly remind you what a *girl boss* she is, which gets a little annoying. David is husband number three and does not seem to understand the concept of drinking in moderation. But I think he's one of those guys who feels the need to do everything to the extreme. Whether it's telling inappropriate-for-children stories about his—not their—amazing life or bragging about another new restaurant that he opened and what celebrities were there—who he probably had to pay to join him.

I know that my mom is a very successful actress, but you never hear her bragging like that. It's just a job she loves to do as opposed to the reason for her existence.

Emery is super laid-back and chill, both in her music and her life, but she smokes like a chimney and spends half her time outside doing so.

Ivery is back in rehab for, like, the fifth time. I feel really sorry that she struggles with addiction, but I guess I just don't understand it. I do know this—I won't be doing any hard drugs. Like, ever.

And it makes me worry that my siblings and I could grow apart. And I wonder if the triplets were ever as close as we are. And I wonder if going away to Eastbrooke and finding our way in the world will pull us apart. I also wonder if that's part of why our parents won't let us go there until next year.

And even though I was going to pester my dad about going next semester, I decide not to. I know their decision wasn't made lightly. And I appreciate that.

Lincoln and Nate are actually really cool and are awesome—and very stylish—parents. And I adore their twins. They are just so enthralled with every little thing. From the ornaments on the tree (which they shouldn't be touching) to Lucky's fur (which they shouldn't be pulling) to the frosting on the cookies (which they shouldn't be crushing on each other's heads).

But I am upset that Aunt Gracie, Uncle Brady, and Waverly didn't come again this year. Waverly and I are in the same grade even though we're about nine months apart, and I just love her. She's got an outrageous personality and a great sense of style.

My ears perk up as I hear Mimi saying something to my mom that sounds a little condescending to my mom, based on her tone. I listen to their conversation, and I realize that Mimi is worried we won't get to relax and enjoy dinner since Mom gave our chef, Marvel, today and tomorrow off to go spend it with his aging parents.

"How's that going to work?" she asks. "Dinner is always a formal affair."

"It will be served differently, but I promise the food will be just as good as always," my mom replies with a forced smile.

I know she worked really hard to get her movie done. And I know even though she's had help around the house, she's still worked tirelessly to give our families and friends an amazing Christmas.

When Mimi goes to refill her cocktail, I walk over to my mom and wrap her in a hug.

"What's that for?" she asks me.

"Thank you for everything you do for us, Mom," I whisper.

"I take it you overheard?"

"Yeah."

"And what do you think?"

"Well, you know the boys would much prefer to have the dinner served family-style, so they don't have to ask to be excused every time they want to go refill their plate."

"Family-style it is then. No reason we can't mix things up once in a while." She gives me a grin. "Your dad told me you want to work at the London Arrington next summer."

"I do. I want to work at *all* of them eventually. But I know you said that Paris was kind of a test. To see if I could handle being away from you guys. Since it was only a few weeks, it wasn't that bad, but if you are okay with it, I'd like to go to the Hamptons with the Johnsons for a two-week summer kickoff and then spend the rest of my break in London."

"Away from Branson?"

"Maybe he could come too? For part of the time?" I offer. That's really what I'm hoping. That we could go together. It would be so much fun to explore the city with him—and possibly romantic.

My mother tilts her head, smiles at me, and then pulls me into a tight hug. "*You* can definitely go to London. You'll have to talk to Branson and his parents about the rest. And of course—"

"There will be rules," I say, finishing her sentence. "And I'm okay with that."

"Good," she says, giving me a kiss.

WE EXCHANGE GIFTS, play some games, and then all freshen up for dinner. Dinner with my mom's family is always a formal affair regardless of how it's served, and I have a super-cute dress to wear. One I wish Branson could see me in.

Then I realize, maybe he can.

> **Me:** *Happy Christmas Eve! I'm trying to decide between two dresses. Help!*
>
> **Branson:** *I'm surprised you're asking me. Usually, you ask Paisley for fashion advice.*

He's referring to Paisley Daniels, who, even though she is a year younger than me, is totally into fashion and wants to be a designer someday. It's not that I don't like fashion, but my taste tends to run more traditional. Paisley teases me that I'll fit right in at Eastbrooke with their plaid skirts and navy blazers—which, even though they are cute, she hates.

> **Me:** *She's at her grandparents' house in Connecticut, and she isn't replying. Surely, you can just tell me if you think they're cute or not. Right?*
> **Branson:** *I guess I can do that.*

The first picture I send him is one of my dress options. It's red velvet with a white Peter Pan collar and a fitted waist, which flares out to a full skirt and hits well below the knee.

> **Branson:** *That's cute. And festive.*
> **Me:** *Okay, here's option two.*

In the next picture I send, I'm in a dress I like better. The top looks like a cable knit cardigan with a fun design featuring little pom-poms, but instead of buttoning up, it simply ties with two thick black ribbon bows in the front, meaning there are glimpses of skin down the center of my chest. It features a banded waist and a skirt that matches the top. And I feel really good in it. Dare I say, a little more grown up. It reminds me of something I would have worn in Paris. I've added simple pearl earrings and black studded booties to go with it.

> **Branson:** *I like the second one the best.*
> **Me:** *Thank you. I like it too.*
> **Branson:** *What are you wearing for New Year's Eve?*
> **Me:** *That is a surprise.*

And it is. Even *I* don't know what my mom got me to wear, and until now, I forgot to ask.

I go back downstairs, put an apron on over the dress, and help my mom and Grandma Arrington set out our traditional prime rib dinner with all the fixings.

Dinner goes well until Avery and David get into a tiff because David won't stop harping on my dad about selling him wine.

She bangs her wineglass down, sloshing a 2008 Reserve Cabernet all over the white tablecloth, and then she gets up and storms off.

David mutters to himself before cursing under his breath and getting up from the table, but he goes out the front door, not the back one she left through.

While all that's going on, for some stupid reason, Emery's boyfriend loudly clinks his wineglass with his fork to get everyone's attention. And what comes out of his mouth shocks me.

"We're out of wine," he says, which seems really rude.

"I'll go grab another bottle," my dad graciously offers.

If I were him, I'd want to punch the guy in the face.

"No, I'd like to do it, if you don't mind," Kenny says, hopping up and away from the table.

Which makes no sense. Why not just let my dad go grab it?

When he comes back with a magnum of wine that is not an Asher Vineyards brand, he places it in front of Emery and says, "Why don't you do the honors?"

and hands her a corkscrew.

She looks at him with the same confused expression we all seem to be wearing and goes, "Uh, sure," as she stands up.

But when she takes the corkscrew in her hands, she finds a long piece of ribbon attached to it. I turn to Monroe, my nose scrunched up in confusion. He just shrugs at me in response.

"What's this?" Emery asks, reeling the long string in. When she gets to the bottom, we all see something shiny tied to it.

"Oh my gosh!" she says, turning to Kenny, only to find him down on one knee next to her.

"So, what do you say, Em? You wanna rock with me forever?"

She starts crying, and I'm not really sure if she's happy or sad, but finally, she flings herself at him and says, "Yes!"

SHORTLY AFTER, THAT side of the family leaves, and Mom, Grandma Arrington and I spend the next hour and a half cleaning up and doing all the dishes. The little kids are yawning, so we put out cookies and milk for Santa and carrots for the reindeers, and then Grandpa Arrington and Doogie take turns reading *'Twas the Night Before Christmas*.

I drop into my bed, exhausted, both physically and emotionally. And I can't stop thinking about the proposal. Which causes me to text Branson.

Me: *Random question of the day.*
Branson: *Shoot.*

Me: *Have you ever thought about what you might say when you propose to your future wife?*

Branson: *Planning to be Mrs. Johnson already?*

Me: *Well, there are plenty of Johnsons to choose from. But that's not what I meant. Aunt Emery got engaged tonight. At dinner. It was weird.*

Branson: *Proposals are supposed to be romantic.*

Me: *I know. Like, it's cool he wanted to propose in front of the family on Christmas Eve and stuff, but right before he did, my aunt Avery got in a fight with her husband, and they both stormed out. The second they were gone, this guy clinked his glass and said we were out of wine. I thought my dad might come unglued because it was just so rude. It's one thing to ask if there is more wine because, I mean, we're on a vineyard, right? There's always more wine. But then he jumped up and offered to go get it. When he got back, he plopped the bottle down in front of my aunt and told her to open it and handed her a corkscrew, like she was some waitress. Then there was a ribbon hanging off the corkscrew, and when she pulled it up, it had an engagement ring attached to it. And he got down on one knee. And guess what he said.*

Branson: *Uh, something like, Will you marry me?*

Me: *Yeah, no. He said, and I quote, "So, what do you say, Em? You wanna rock with me forever?"*

Branson: *Well, he's a drummer in her backup band, right? So, I suppose maybe he thought that was clever.*

Me: *Do you think it was clever?*

Branson: *It sounds kinda lame to me, honestly. My parents wouldn't want me to say that to my future wife, I don't think.*

Me: *Good, because you shouldn't. But maybe I'm*

being too harsh. She looked really happy. Of course, the ring was pretty impressive.

Branson: Big?

Me: Huge but also funky. The ring is the one thing he did right. It was very much her style. Multiple chunky stones. She loved it.

Branson: That's all that matters then, right?

Me: Yeah. I guess. I think it was the "rock with me" part. It sounded cheesy. And maybe that made it feel insincere.

Branson: Don't girls like cheesy love stories? But. . . I will say that tonight, I kept thinking of you in that dress. Actually, when I looked at the picture again, Beck saw it, stole my phone, and was saying that you looked pretty hot.

Me: Really? Did he mean it or was he joking?

Branson: He meant it. And he's right, Laney. You did look really nice.

Nice wasn't exactly what I was going for, but I suppose it's close enough.

Me: Thanks. All right, it's getting late. And you know what they say, Santa won't come until I go to sleep.

Branson: Beck stole my phone and made a dirty comment, which I won't repeat, but it was along the lines of what he'd do if he were there before you went to sleep. Also, it's almost morning here. You always forget we're three hours later here on the East Coast.

Me: Crap. You're right. I always do. Well, I'm glad you were awake to talk to me.

Branson: Me too. Night, Laney.

December 25th

VERY, VERY GOOD.
KEATYN

I'M LIKE A kid on Christmas morning, and I can never sleep the night before. But because I remember the excitement, I always pretend to be asleep when the kids come in to wake us up.

Last night felt like a bit of a disaster with my family, but Emery was really excited about getting engaged, and I was happy both for them and the festive feel it lent to the occasion. Avery and David seemed to make up quickly after their spat and were all snuggly and lovey with each other the rest of the evening.

I hear the pitter-patter of little feet heading toward our door. Aiden, who I didn't think was awake yet, touches the side of my leg and pretends to snore loudly.

I sneak my head under the covers but leave an opening, so I can see them come into our room. Not surprisingly, it's the younger two, Steele and Arden.

They are dressed in their matching flannel jammies, and I snap a memory picture in my head.

It was hard to walk away from Hollywood years ago. A lot of people thought we were crazy. Suggested that it would never work. That no one would want to be part of it. But they did. Sure, sometimes, like this week, we had to work overtime to complete a project, but we did it for a reason. So that we could have a full three weeks off before starting post-production, and so we could enjoy time off with those we wanted to spend it with.

But being home with my children, having my "set" basically at my house, was the ultimate work from home for all of us. And when the world changed and more were forced to work remotely, we already had everything in place.

And it's moments like these—not just holidays, but every day, of time spent watching in amazement as our babies grow—that make it all worth it. And I know I don't have too many more years of Arden really believing in Santa. It's part of why Aiden has gone a little over the top with her birthday party tomorrow. He's literally created Santa's workshop with a carnival feel. We always decorate with a theme for Christmas with our friends, but this year, he's gone all out.

"Daddy is snoring," Arden whisper-giggles to her brother.

"Shh. Let's jump on the bed and scare them," Steele whispers back.

Together, they leap on the bed. Aiden is ready for

them though, opening his eyes and grabbing them midair as they do, causing them to both scream out loud.

"Ahhh!"

"Caught you," Aiden says. "Why are you up so early?"

"Because it's Christmas, Daddy," Arden says very seriously. She's also looking at him like he's slightly crazy for not knowing this.

"Oh, that's right! I wonder if Santa was here last night."

"He was!" she yells out. "The cookies, milk, and carrots are gone, our stockings are full, and there are new presents under the tree. One for each of us!"

"Well, you must have been good, huh?"

She nods enthusiastically. "I was very, very good. Because I want Santa to bring me a pony."

"Was there a pony-sized gift under the tree?" Aiden banters.

She shakes her little head, looking disappointed. "No."

"Well, should we go out there and open yours now to see?"

"No, Daddy! We have to wait for everyone to get up first. That's what you always say."

"He does always say that," Steele agrees.

"Then you two had better go wake everyone up! And don't forget your grandparents."

"Yay!" they scream, hopping off the bed and racing out of the room.

I throw the covers off, and Aiden goes, "You're

fully dressed and ready."

"I have been for a couple hours! I'm pretty sure I'm more excited than the kids."

"Arden is going to be beside herself when she opens the saddle Santa got her."

"Especially once she finds out that her Doogie bought her a pony," I add. "Come on. I'll put the breakfast casseroles in the oven and heat up the hot chocolate. You get a fire going and text Grandpa and tell him it's time."

WHAT IS MY ANSWER?
AUBREY LANE

I LOVE CHRISTMAS morning. Sure, the presents are really fun, but we also do a crazy Saran Wrap thing, where Dad puts small items that can be anything from trinkets to silly gag gifts to big gift cards into a ball. We open our presents from each other and our parents, then do the Saran Wrap thing, and then a crazy white elephant gift exchange, where I have to steal something my brother wants so I can barter with him to win the cute beaded bracelet I want back from my mom.

We have a leisurely brunch and then open our gifts from Santa. I'm excited to find my first ever designer handbag. I know my mom has a closet full of them and that I could probably borrow one if I ever wanted to, but she always said I needed to wait until I was older to get one of my own. It's so pretty, and it's purple, which is my favorite color. Maybe not totally practical, but I don't care. The leather is soft and supple, and I want to carry it around all day long, like I did whenever I got a new baby doll when I was little.

Usually, the Santa gifts are opened in age order from youngest to oldest. And when that long-standing tradition is switched up from oldest to youngest this year, I know something is up.

"Finally, it's my turn!" Arden yells before ripping into the paper on her gift.

Everyone knows she wanted a pony this year. Actually, she's wanted her *very own* pony for about the last four years, but our parents told her she had to wait until she was old enough to help take care of it. And obviously, they don't think she's ready yet since the box is clearly not big enough to hold a horse.

"It's beautiful," she says when she gets the box open and peers inside.

None of us can see what it is, but she looks mesmerized and a little teary-eyed.

"What is it, Arden?" Monroe asks her.

"It's my very own saddle!" she calls out as Monroe goes over to help her get it out of the box.

Aspen grabs a nearby wooden bench, and together, they put the saddle on top of it. Arden starts clapping and hops on it.

"I wanted a pony really, really badly, but I must not be old enough yet," she says in an adorable little voice. "But when I do get one, I'll have a beautiful saddle to ride it with." She looks up at the sky and says, "Thank you, Santa Claus."

Doogie gets up from his chair by the fire and says, "Or maybe Santa is in cahoots with your Doogie."

"What does ca-hoots mean?" she asks him.

And I know exactly what it means. *Doogie* must have bought her a horse.

"It means, I told him what I got you for your birthday, so he got you something to go with it as your Christmas gift. I mean, it would be kind of hard to get a pony in his sleigh," Doogie tells her.

Tears fill her little eyes. "Doogie got me a pony?"

He picks her up and hugs her. "I did. Do you want to go meet her and see what you think?"

"Yes!!"

Arden's reaction is amazing, and it reminds me of how happy I was when I got Sparky. My mom has had her phone out, snapping pictures and taking videos like crazy.

Dad grabs the saddle and asks the boys to help him get it in one of the golf carts for the trip down to the stables.

Mom and I hop in her cart and she's clearly on a mission.

"You're going a little fast," I tease.

"I want to get there first, so I can record everything."

"Why don't you let me do that, Mom? You're always telling us to live in the moment and not behind a camera. So, live in it."

Mom turns to me and smiles. "Wow. You actually listen to me once in a while."

"I listen to you all the time. You know that."

"I do. But I like that you're your own woman. That will be important as you grow up. And especially when you leave more often."

"Like going to London?"

"That, and Eastbrooke next year. There are a lot of ways kids can get into trouble. Things they can do that adversely affect not only their own lives, but also others' lives."

"I'm never doing drugs, Mom. I don't want a life like Aunt Ivery's."

"I know that. It's just, sometimes, it's easy to get caught up in stuff."

"Is that why you've been making us wait? You don't trust us?"

"It's not that at all, sweetie. Honestly, it's probably more about me than it is about you. I'm not ready for you to leave. To not see you every day. And I didn't start until my junior year, and I still made a ton of friends. And I hope you will too."

"We already know a lot of people who go there, so I don't think it will be hard. Did you know anyone when you went?"

She shakes her head. "No, I didn't."

And the way she says it makes me wonder what she isn't telling me. There's something about when she went to Eastbrooke or was there that gives her pause about sending us.

"You loved it there, right?" I ask her.

"I very much did. And I loved your dad from the moment I saw him, but there are a lot of tough choices to make when you're on your own like that. Branson's dad's first wife—"

"Ava and Harlow's mom?"

"Yes. Her name was Whitney, and she was considered the most popular girl there."

"Why do I feel like there's a *but*?"

"Because if you didn't know better, you would have thought she had the perfect life. She was popular, beautiful, and came from a wealthy family. But that family put a ton of pressure on her to succeed, and I think she just never felt good enough."

"Branson told me she committed suicide when his sisters were young."

"Yes. And the first time she tried was her senior year at Eastbrooke."

"Wow. That's really sad."

"It is. And I know that sometimes, I don't treat you like the young adult you are becoming. I'm so incredibly proud of you, Aubrey Lane. Your work ethic. Your intelligence. Even your sassiness. And I know you'll do great there. And I know you were mad at me for not letting you go before, but I wanted to make sure you were ready."

"So, any chance I could go this January?" I figure I might as well strike while the iron is hot.

"No way," she says with a grin as we pull up in front of the stables.

I give her a hug. "I love you. Now, let's go see this horse!"

I'M SITTING ON the fence, watching Arden happily ride her horse around the corral. So far, they seem to be a good match. And I don't think I've ever seen her smile so big.

Doogie comes to stand next to me. "She reminds me of you."

I look at him. "She reminds me of Grammy. She had such a lust for life that it was practically contagious. I miss her. Especially today."

"I have something for you," Doogie says.

"Did you get me a pony too?" I tease.

"No." He hands me a small black velvet box. "Go ahead and open it."

Nestled in the fabric is a necklace. A necklace that I've been fascinated with since I was a little girl and Grammy told me the story about how Doogie picked her daisies and gave them to her on their first date. Tears prickle my eyes. She wore this necklace every single day. Doogie is rich and he bought Grammy beautiful jewelry over the years, but this and her wedding ring were what she wore every day.

"She wanted you to have it," he says, taking it out of the box, putting it around my neck, and fastening it.

I hold the daisy charm in my hand and say, "This is way better than a pony. Thank you. I will cherish it forever."

Doogie looks a little misty-eyed when he says, "That means a lot to me. I love you, Lane."

I jump into his arms. "I love you too, Doogie."

ONCE ALL THE excitement is over, we go back home and relax. I take my gifts up to my room and decide to text Branson.

>*Me:* Get anything good?
>
>*Branson:* I'd rather YOU give me something good.
>
>*Me:* Uh, I haven't given you your present yet. But of course it's good. I mean, I think you'll like it. You usually do.
>
>*Branson:* Does it involve us being naked?

Uh . . . *what?*
We went from a NYE kiss to naked?
Wait a second . . .

>*Me:* OMG, Beck, or whichever Johnson has hijacked Branson's phone, you know it's not like that.
>
>*Branson:* Maybe it should be.
>
>*Me:* Did he tell you that's what he wants, or are you just being your usual annoying self?
>
>*Branson:* Guess who this is.
>
>*Me:* I already guessed—Beckham.
>
>*Branson:* When are you coming to Eastbrooke already? Poor Branson was dateless at the dance. And it was embarrassing. We Johnsons have a reputation to uphold.
>
>*Me:* I hope you know that I'm rolling my eyes right now.
>
>*Branson:* Come on. Don't you like Branson? He's not as good-looking as me, but you know . . .
>
>*Me:* I know. He's a Johnson. You all think you're God's gifts to women.
>
>*Branson:* Pretty sure we are. So, if you don't want to play with him, I'm sorta single.
>
>*Me:* Sorta single? Either you are or you aren't.
>
>*Branson:* Eh . . . I've got a girl, but she's not THE

girl.

Me: *But I could be?*

Branson: *Why not?*

Me: *Beck, do you like it at Eastbrooke? Like, do you love it? Don't you miss your family? My mom just told me that I could go for sure next fall. If I want to. Do I want to?*

Branson: *Uh, yeah, you do. 1. Your brothers will be with you. 2. Your boy Beck is there. And when you're with me, a good time is guaranteed.*

Me: *If you know what I mean. Wink-wink, right?*

Oh my gosh. Is Beck flirting with me? And did I sort of just flirt back?

Branson: *Hey, love that you thought of it first. Seriously, get your ass to school.*

Me: *I will. But in the meantime, YOU should come to our NYE party this year.*

Branson: *So we can kiss at midnight? Isn't that what every girl wants? To be kissed by a Johnson at midnight?*

Yeah, I think.

Me: *It is a romantic thought.*

Branson: *I can do romance.*

Me: *Bahahahaha.*

Branson: *That hurts. Are you serious? Do you want me to be there?*

Me: *Of course.*

Branson: *Lane.*

Me: *Am I dying to kiss YOU at midnight? Is that your question?*

Branson: *Yes. What's your answer? If I'm flying all*

the way out there . . .

And I mean, Beck is hot with a capital *H*. And I love him . . . but he's not Branson.

Branson: *OMG. It's Branson for real this time. I'm sorry. Beck stole my phone while I was playing pool with Uncle Cam. Wait. What was your answer going to be? And were you flirting with him?*

What is my answer? I close my eyes. Think of them both.

Beckham is just plain fun to be around. The kind of guy who would talk you into doing all the things your mother warned you about. The kind of guy who could clearly teach you a thing or two about life and love and then would probably break your heart because he's easily distracted.

Specifically by butts—shapely ones. And when you're on the beach with him and you have a more athletic shape, as in a little more straight up and down than curvy, and are treated like one of the guys, that can be . . . a little devastating. I used to have a crush on Beck. He's only a year older, but he's always seemed more mature than me and Branson. He's definitely more experienced. And he's got that playful, naughty thing going on—not quite the bad boy, yet certainly no angel.

And then there's my Branson.

Sweet, adorable Branson, who doesn't quite fit the Johnson mold. No tattoos. No constant parade of girls in and out of his life.

And the one I might sorta be in love with.

Me: I wasn't going to reply to that, honestly, because I knew he was just messing with me.

Branson: I'm gonna go kick his ass now.

Me: Why?

Branson: One, I would never say those things to you.

Why not?

Branson: And two, he needs to stop flirting with my girl.

Me: Your girl?

Branson: I mean, like, I have dibs on you.

Me: You what?

Branson: Like, he knows I like you.

Me: You do?

Branson: Of course I do. You're my best friend.

And therein lies the problem.

Me: Except you said you wanted to kiss me on NYE. That it would mean I'd be yours all year.

Branson: And I hope your answer to Beck is— DON'T COME TO THE PARTY.

Me: I mean, he's fun to hang out with.

Branson: Just don't encourage him. He's got his phone now. And he's texting and giving me a smirk. He's texting you, isn't he?

Beck: What's the verdict? NYE kiss or not?

Me: Who knows?

Me: *Yes, he just texted me.*

Branson: *Say no.*

Beck: *Playing coy. Love it.*

Me: *Of course you would.*

Beck: *I'll get back to you.*

Me: *Why don't you just surprise me?*

Beck: *Deal. I do have other plans, but now, we'll see.*

Me: *Figures.*

Beck: *What can I say? I'm in demand.*

Branson: *What did you say to him?*

Me: *Well, I can't exactly uninvite him. His family has a standing invite. You all do.*

Branson: *True. Well, I gotta go. See you tomorrow. And, Laney?*

Me: *Yeah?*

Branson: *Merry Christmas!*

Me: *Merry Christmas to you too.*

I flop back on my bed, wondering what exactly just transpired.

Was Beck flirting with me just to mess with Branson?

And if so, will it make Branson a little jealous and more likely to want to kiss me on our ski trip?

Inquiring minds want to know.

And by inquiring, I mean, me.

December 26th

STILL WAITING.
AUBREY LANE

TODAY'S THE WINTER wonderland carnival for Arden's birthday and a celebration with our closest friends.

I've just finished dressing in my Cindy-Lou Who costume when Branson texts me to say he's pulling up to our house.

The best part is, that means he hasn't even gone home and is getting dropped off to see me first.

I'm barely out the front door when strong arms pull me into a hug. Seriously, he always gives me the best hugs, and I usually just soak them in.

But this time, it feels a little awkward.

Because Beckham is standing behind him, a smirk on his face and his eyebrows raised in a challenging way. And when it's his turn to greet me, he does it in a big fashion—pulling me off my feet and twirling me around dramatically.

Which makes me laugh, even as I say, "Beck, put

me down!"

He does as requested, stopping immediately.

But he doesn't let go of me. I'm still in his arms, my chest flattened against his, our bodies melded together. And when he releases me, my body does a slow-motion slide down the front of him.

I look up at him, our eyes locking in the moment, which makes it feel even more intimate.

And I'm not sure how long it actually takes him to let go of me, but the process leaves me a little shook. Although Branson and I have been BFFs forever, I've been friends with both of them basically since I was born. Beck and his family come out here for holidays or my family goes to their summer place in the Hamptons.

But this feels different. I feel out of breath and my body is humming. Like it wants to be pressed back against him. *Him!* As in Beck. And I don't even *like* him.

But it doesn't help that he's now staring at my mouth, looking like he might want to kiss me. Could Beck *want* to kiss me?

"So," Branson says loudly, "what's the birthday party theme this year?"

"Uh," I stutter in an attempt to get my brain to form a sentence. "Uh, winter wonderland."

"Sounds fun," Branson says flatly, looking irritated, possibly by whatever it was that just transpired between Beck and me.

"It should be." I try to make things better by wrapping my arms around their shoulders and say,

"Let's go down to the barn and sneak some cookies."

Branson yells, "Last one there is a rotten egg!"

They both take off running, causing my arms to fall to my sides and leaving me wondering what's going to happen next. Because Branson has never hugged me the way Beck just did.

MY PARENTS LOVE to host big events. Whether it's weddings for friends, fundraising galas for Moon Wish wines, or family celebrations, they tend to do it up big. I know we live in a really nice house, travel in our own plane, and have houses in Paris and London, but these events are always a splurge. Over the top. Crazy fun. But this year feels about ten levels up.

First, they installed a new gorgeous glass-paneled structure outside the back of the barn. It reminds me of a large conservatory. It and the barn are decorated to look like a mini North Pole. There are animatronic elves making toys and baking cookies. Wreaths and garland cover all the beams. And even a little town scene is outside with food truck vendors set up, serving treats you'd expect to find where Santa lives. There's traditional stuff, like cookies and warm drinks, but also snowmen-shaped pizzas and other holiday fare. There are craft-making tables with craftsmen and women dressed up in festive garb and a whole section of holiday-themed carnival games with prizes, like stuffed reindeer and Santas. Our Ferris wheel is offering rides. There's a snow machine going, covering the area with snow even though it isn't cold enough here for it to last very long. A huge Santa's workshop–

decorated birthday cake, featuring prancing ponies on the top. And the pièce de resistance—an ice skating rink inside the glass structure, which has been cooled to below freezing.

It's amazing. And so much fun.

The birthday girl is on cloud nine.

I spend some time skating with Beck. He plays hockey at Eastbrooke and is good on the ice, so he teaches me how to twirl in circles.

And later, Branson and I grab hot chocolates, warm brownies, and pink cotton candy and get driven around the property in the horse-drawn carriage that looks like Santa's sleigh.

Hanging out with both boys is great, but things start to feel a little romantic when Branson puts his arm around my shoulders.

We talk a ton.

Laugh.

Comment on the stars.

But let's just say, I'm *still* waiting for a kiss.

December 30th

A LITTLE CRAZY.
KEATYN

VANESSA, ARIELA, AND I meet up in the gazebo overlooking the pond early this morning for coffee and catching up.

"How is the Johnson family doing?" I ask.

It's kind of crazy to me that Vanessa lives out here. She had a gorgeous estate in Holmby Hills that she redid when Dawson and his girls moved in with her. All was good until about nine years ago when one of her PR clients was embroiled in a legal situation involving injuries at one of his live music events. The scandal became so blown up in the press, so big, that it sucked in everyone who had anything to do with the performer. Including Vanessa.

One day, the paparazzi was waiting for her when she went to pick up Branson, who was only six at the time, from school. And when she got home, there were more who had managed to breach her gated property. And that was when she was done. She didn't pack a thing. She had her family on a plane bound for Sonoma, and they stayed in one of our guesthouses until they purchased their own property and built a house here.

Dallas and RiAnne are the only ones who still live in the city, but they love their country-club life, and although we've added a lot of amenities here for all of us—like a community pool, tennis courts, and equestrian center—a golf course isn't one of them.

And I understand why Vanessa reacted the way she did. It's why we've kept the kids out here for the most part. We still have our houses in London and Paris, but we sold the New York and the Malibu beach houses a few years ago. All of The Arringtons that have been built since the triplets arrived feature a large penthouse suite, where we stay when we are in town, and with so many of them around the world to choose from, there's no need to own separate homes.

And as one would expect after my experience with a stalker, I'm overly protective. Although many celebrities flaunt pictures of their children on social media, I won't allow it or let them come to premieres or events where they would be photographed. Moving out here so they could live a normal life was the smartest thing Aiden and I have ever done.

"Good," Vanessa says. "We had a nice time. Although it's always a little crazy with so many people around."

"And there was the engagement!" Ariela adds.

"We had an engagement too. Tell me yours was better. And who was it?" I ask.

"Do you remember Ransom, one of Riley's older cousins?" Ariela asks.

"Of course I remember him. He's what, about four years older than Riley? And he's the one who donated the beer bong to the party shed, if I recall."

"Yes, he was. He's still proud of that, and he reminds everyone every time we are together," Vanessa says with a laugh.

"Anyway," Ariela continues, "it was his son, Blake. He's been dating the girl for a couple years now. They met at medical school, will graduate in the spring, and want to get married right away so they can do their residencies together."

"And?" I ask. I love the romantic details.

"Well, we were doing our version of a white elephant exchange, and she chose the package with the ring—literally, I have no idea how he rigged it so she chose the right gift."

"Oh, I do," Vanessa says. "It was gift number eight, her favorite number."

"That's sweet," I offer.

"Anyway, it was a custom stethoscope," Vanessa says. "Obviously, a gift for her and one she would have fought tooth and nail to keep, but no one else probably would have wanted it."

"And it was so funny," Ariela adds, "because she was so enthralled, checking it out, that she didn't even notice for the longest time that something else was in the box. She was sitting there, putting it on, listening to her own heartbeat. Taking it off and studying it closer. She had no clue the game had stopped and

Blake was down on one knee in front of her."

"Oh my gosh! I love it!"

"Finally," Vanessa says, "Blake's like, *Hey, there's something else in the box. An accessory for it, I think.* So she opens the box and is shocked to find a ring. She started crying, and he went into this whole thing about how his heart beats faster ever since the day they met and how his heart now beats for her."

"I loved it," Ariela says. "And I hope they ask me to plan their wedding. There are so many cute things we could do to personalize it."

"How about yours?" Vanessa asks. "Who got engaged?"

"Emery. To Kenny."

"The drummer from her band, right? They've dated, what, a couple months?" Ariela says.

"Like, six. But she seems happy. It was weird though." I tell them about what happened right before. How he didn't wait for Avery and David to come back. And what he said.

"Rock with me. Huh," Ariela says. "Well, it fits. Was she happy? That's all that really matters."

"I think so."

"Well, I don't know about you all, but I'm ready for Riley and Mason to get back home from Tahoe. Have some quiet family time," Ariela says.

"Except for the whole New Year's Eve bash you put together," I tease.

"Oh, that. I could do that in my sleep. It will be fun though."

"I'm glad you're both back home," I tell them. "I

missed our coffee time."

"Us too," Vanessa says.

LIKE ONE OF THE GUYS.
AUBREY LANE

WE WERE UP at the crack of dawn, and when we get home from our ski trip, it's well before noon. My brothers and I drop all of our ski gear and luggage on the mudroom floor to be dealt with later.

Monroe says, "I need a nap."

"Ditto," Aspen says.

"You guys can't keep up, huh?" I tease, knowing they are tired from skiing nonstop for days as well as being a little hungover.

"Hey, you didn't ski as much as we did," Aspen argues.

"Because I went shopping *one* day. Big deal. I can keep up with you. It's not like you even drank until last night."

Ski all day and drink all night was their plan, but after you've skied all day, you're exhausted, and they barely got through a late dinner before dropping into bed.

But last night they managed to stay up and play a drinking game after Riley went to sleep.

I feel great because *I* didn't partake in the game. I'm smart enough to know not to try to outdrink a bunch of boys.

And although I do enjoy a glass of wine with

dinner on occasion, my nightly ritual includes a steaming cup of mint tea and a couple squares of dark chocolate.

Which all the boys teased me about.

And when I say boys, I mean it. I ended up being the only girl, surrounded by my brothers and a bunch of Johnson cousins—six to be exact. The three older cousins had fake IDs, which allowed them to sneak into clubs, so I mostly hung out with my brothers, Branson, Beck, and Mason, who had just turned fourteen and was on his first kids' ski trip.

I think about Mason's mom and dad, Riley and Ariela. How they dated in high school, spent ten years apart, and then made their way back to one another.

I think about stuff like that a lot. Relationships. How they work.

Probably because I'm mostly wondering when or if I'll ever have one myself.

And I will admit, I had big ideas for this trip regarding me and Branson. Especially after his texts and us discussing the possibility of being more than friends.

Of kissing.

Of us hanging out together in *my* bed.

But then, nothing.

And I mean, *zero* happened.

No knowing glances.

No playful flirting.

Not even an accidental brush of his hand across mine.

Honestly, he treated me like one of the guys.

And worse, like one of his cousins.

I don't understand how he could talk about us kissing and dating just a few days ago, and then when we finally had all sorts of opportunities for things to happen *and* were away from our parents, he acted like the conversation never occurred.

And I really wished some of the girls had come. Especially Farryn McMahon. She lives in LA, is a year older than me, and has dated quite a few guys. She could have given me some advice. But she canceled when her sister Fallon had her first baby the day we left.

Beck, on the other hand, did flirt with me a little.

And I appreciated it.

But I think it was mostly in pity. He only seemed to bring up New Year's Eve when Branson was around, and he never tried to hang out with me alone—even when I offered up a little shopping trip in town as bait.

Nope. It was off to the slopes.

You always hear that boys have one-track minds. Usually referring to sex.

In my case, however, it was all about the diamonds. Black ones particularly. And in this situation, they were *not* a girl's best friend.

I DECIDE TO change clothes, freshen up, and then go see if I can track down the part of my family that is not sleeping in the middle of the afternoon. Honestly, I was a little surprised no one greeted us when we got home. But I suspect they are probably prepping for the

New Year's Eve party tomorrow night.

I'm heading back downstairs when I get a text.

Beck: *Well, I did it. But I'm bored already. Wanna hang out?*

Me: *Did what?*

Beck: *Sent my brothers home without me.*

Me: *You stayed?*

Beck: *Yep. And I'm already regretting my decision. Branson passed out the second we got here, and Aunt Vanessa and Uncle Dawson are nowhere to be found.*

Me: *Same goes for my family. I think they are all at the barn, doing party prep. I was about to have a snack. You hungry?*

Beck: *If you were a normal girl, I'd say yes. FOR YOU. Especially if your parents aren't home.*

Me: *"Gee, thanks," says the NOT-normal girl in reply.*

Beck: *I am actually starving. Come get me, so I don't have to walk.*

Me: *Just steal Branson's golf cart. You know where the keys are.*

Beck: *Yeah, usually, I do. I think he hid them from me, so I wouldn't hang out with you while he slept.*

Me: *Doubtful. He's not interested in me like that. I think that's pretty obvious.*

Beck: *Well, he had his chance in Tahoe. He struck out.*

Me: *You can't strike out unless you step up to the plate. It's like he forfeited.*

Beck: *Either way. Come get me.*

Me: *You're an athlete, Beck. Run. It will give me time to make food.*

Beck: *Come get me. We'll cook together. And I guarantee it will be hot in the kitchen.*

Me: *You and your lines. Fine. I'll be right there.*

I look up and realize that I've been standing here this whole time, texting Beck, with the refrigerator door open, so I quickly shut it. My heart races as I grab a set of keys with my name on them off the rack in the mudroom and go to the golf cart garage.

When my brothers and I turned fourteen, we each got a custom golf cart to drive around The Enclave. I move past Monroe's—a red two-seater, the body modeled after the Ferrari F5 Spider. It's flashy, and it attracts attention, just like he does. Aspen is the most social of the three of us, so his black California Roadster limo style seats all us kids comfortably and has a luxurious feel. Mine is somewhere in between. A four-seater based off my dad's favorite car—a pearlized white Maserati that he's had since he was, like, seventeen or something. Since he and I are a lot alike, I think he knew I'd love it.

And I do.

AS I'M FOLLOWING the golf path to Branson's house, I start to get nervous.

Because what *would* I do if Beck tried to kiss me? Like, really? Would I kiss him back, or do I owe Branson some sort of allegiance?

Why, oh why, didn't Branson act like he liked me when we were skiing? Was he embarrassed to do anything while around his cousins? Embarrassed of me?

Or did he change his mind and decide that we should

just continue along as friends?

I glance in the rearview mirror at myself. I've grown out of what I call my gawky phase—when I was growing tall and lacked the coordination I used to have. My mom liked to dance, so all of us kids have been in classes pretty much since we could walk. But there was a period where I just felt like my feet were too big and my body was awkward. I don't think my mother ever went through a phase like that, but my dad's sister—my aunt Peyton—said *she* did. That it's normal. And I can't help but wonder if my brain is still stuck in it somehow even though my body has grown out of it.

Stuck in the friend zone.

One I don't know how to get out of.

When I get close to Branson's house, I see that Beck is waiting for me at the end of their long driveway. He's got on a pair of jeans, dark brown leather high-tops, a red ball cap turned backward, and his Eastbrooke letterman's jacket. Beck is a three-sport athlete—lacrosse, hockey, and baseball—but his favorite is baseball. And when he looks in my direction, his dark eyes sparkling with excitement, I maybe swoon a little even though I don't like him like that.

"Why have I not seen this golf cart before?" he asks, causing me to realize it wasn't actually me that he was looking at.

That's it. No more being friends with boys.

I look down at myself and roll my eyes.

Yes, I freshened up and changed clothes, but I'm

dressed in my usual jeans, cowboy boots, and a flannel shirt with a puffer vest over the top, and I have my hair held in a simple braid. Mostly because I thought I might take Sparky out for a ride if nothing else was going on.

"Because you haven't been out here since we got them," I offer.

"Them?" he questions.

"Monroe and Aspen got custom golf carts too. I think they were partially guilt gifts because our parents didn't let us go to Eastbrooke freshman year, as planned."

"Totally sucks. We'd be having so much fun together."

"Do you think?" I shrug my shoulders noncommittally, like I don't care even though I sort of do. In fact, that sounded kind of flirty.

"Of course I think," Beck says, flipping my braid. "Lane, you don't have to have your life all planned out just yet. I love that you have big aspirations and want to be a hotel mogul—"

"Who told you that?" I say, my eyes big. I really haven't told anyone that, except . . .

"Branson. He's proud of you."

I let out a sigh. First, he ignored me on our ski trip, and then he betrayed my trust.

"Awesome," is all I say.

"I HAVE A plan," Beck says, giving me a devilish grin once we're in my kitchen, standing in front of the open fridge.

"What kind of plan?"

"Let's make lunch, take it down to the soccer field, and then kick the ball around."

"Okay, cool. That sounds fun."

We pack up provisions, piling them into a picnic basket, and then go back outside and to the soccer field.

Beck grabs the blanket I threw in at the last minute, spreading it out in the middle of the field.

"This reminds me of Eastbrooke," he says as we take a seat, get our food out, and chitchat while we eat.

Once we're finished, he grabs a soccer ball out of the cart and kicks it toward me.

"So, what are you going to do when you come to Eastbrooke?"

"What do you mean?" I ask, dribbling the ball down the field toward him and then passing it off.

"Like sports. Activities."

"Is partying an activity?" I tease, knowing that's probably more what he's referring to.

Beck's face breaks out into a wide grin. "If it were, I'd letter in that."

"Can you even party there?" I ask him. "Like, my mom's always telling me about the strict rules they have. Which doesn't make it sound that fun sometimes. I mean, if I want to go outside at midnight and stare at the stars here, I can. Apparently, you can't do that there."

He picks up the soccer ball and bounces it off his knees a couple of times, and then he pops it up in my direction.

I catch it and stand there as he moves closer to me.

He puts his hands over mine, like he's helping me hold the ball, and shakes his head. "There are ways around curfew."

"What do you mean? I thought bells went off and alarms sounded or something."

"That's why God made windows, Lane."

"Are you saying that you sneak out the window?" Now, I think I understand what my mom meant about me having to make decisions about these kinds of things.

"That's what I'm saying."

"And it's allowed?"

He squeezes my hands as he breaks out in laughter. Like he thinks I'm hilarious. He steals the ball from me, drops it on the ground, and takes off down the field. I chase after him, not wanting to let him score, and luckily, I'm fast. I get in front of him before he reaches the goal. I kick the ball away, but our feet get tangled up, and we both go to the ground, me landing on top of him.

"You've always been faster than us boys," he says, grinning at me, but then his hands slide from just under my butt to over the top of it and up my back. And it's like when he slid me down his body after greeting me the other day. It causes my cheeks to flush, like I'm coming down with a fever.

Or maybe I'm slightly lovesick.

Because the person I wish were touching me like this is not Beck.

Actually, I think there's a story line like this in a

script my mom has been working on recently. The girl is best friends with one brother but has a thing for his older brother. Of course, it's not finished yet, so I don't know how the story will end. Will she fall for the hot older cousin—uh, I mean, brother—or the friend one?

I tilt my head upward, staring at his handsome face. I will admit, he is very good-looking. And just when I wonder what it would be like to kiss him, he growls at me, does a snapping thing with his teeth like he's going to bite me, jumps up, races toward the ball, and kicks it into the goal.

While he's leaping up and down in victory, I'm still lying on the ground, thinking about the fact that I just considered kissing someone besides Branson.

Beck comes to stand over me, his legs straddling either side of me. "Are you okay?" he asks, concern written all over his face.

I raise my eyebrows at him and then bring my leg up between his, stopping just short of racking him.

He reacts by crouching and grabbing his crotch, trying to protect himself, which makes me laugh.

"Oh, you think that's funny, huh?" he says and then leaps on top of me.

We roll around on the ground, him trying to pin me in a wrestling move and me trying to escape.

"I think you missed the whole point of this exercise," he says, his hair shagging in his dark eyes as he leans over me.

"What *point* are you referring to?" I ask, thinking if I was smart, I'd flirt with him. But the truth is, I really don't know how.

He goes, "I lead. You follow."

And I don't follow.

I mean, I'd probably follow him around, but I'm not currently following his train of thought. Mostly because he's practically lying on top of me again.

"When you get to Eastbrooke," he clarifies, "just follow my lead. I'll show you how to sneak out without getting caught."

"And what will we do when we sneak out?" I ask, trying to sound a little flirtatious. Maybe I just need a little practice at it.

"You know, party."

"*But I always say, one's company, two's a crowd, and three's a party*," I say, quoting Andy Warhol.

He grins. "Shit. I like that. It's like a pick-up line. Laneybug-a-boo-boo-bear, are you trying to pick me up?"

I press my lips together. "You're a Johnson. It's hard to know what that mind of yours is thinking. What kind of partying are we talking about?"

He pops up off the ground, pulling me up with him. "I'm talking, smoking, drinking, dancing, and the inevitable pairing up."

"Like boys and girls?"

"If that's what you're into. But yes. Pairing up is a less threatening way of saying hooking up. No sex implied, just chatting, you know—unless the girl wants more. And thankfully, she usually does."

"I doubt anyone will want to pair up with me, and besides, I wouldn't want to get in trouble. Can you imagine me, an Arrington, getting kicked out? Our last name is on the school's chapel!"

"Don't forget the library," he adds with a smirk.

"You know what I mean."

"Actually, I don't," he says. "Because you're very wrong about one thing."

"What's that?" I ask him.

"Your green eyes are mesmerizing, and you're gorgeous, Lane."

"I'm sure there are a lot of pretty girls at East-brooke," I counter.

"True." He gives me a wink. Kisses my cheek. Pulls on my braid. "Like I said, I'll lead. You follow."

"I'd have to trust you for that."

"You'd better trust me," he says. "And worst case, my uncle is the dean. It's not like we're going to get kicked out."

"Fair point."

He glances at his watch. "Okay, shit. I gotta get back to the house. We're doing a family video conference for my grandma's birthday. See ya later."

I PLOP BACK down on the blanket, lie back, and stare up at the wispy clouds floating lazily across the sky.

And I wonder if I am crushing on the wrong boy.

But my heart seems to think it's a silly question. Like, you can't help who you like.

Am I confusing my friendship with Branson as something more?

No, I'm not crazy. I know he likes me. He told me so. And he never lies to me. Maybe he didn't want to kiss me when his family was around or something.

I consider my shooting-star wish and how tomorrow is the last day of the year. And how if my wish doesn't come true, I'll be really sad.

But I also know that at some point I'm going to have to give up hope on us ever being more than just friends.

EVENTUALLY, I GO back to my house.

Where I'm surprised to find Branson waiting for me in my room.

I sit down next to him on my bed.

"I haven't given you your present yet," he says.

"I know. I'm excited to give you yours. When do you want to do our exchange?"

"How about tonight? Could we do something together? Just us? I miss you. Miss the two of us just always hanging out."

"I do too. And yes, tonight. What should we do?"

His eyes meet mine, and he slowly blinks as a smile spreads across his face. "Leave that to me."

"What do you have planned?" I ask because it's now obvious he's already got something in mind.

He leans his head against mine, our foreheads touching sweetly as he takes my hands in his. "I'll pick you up at seven."

"Where are we going?" I question.

He grins again. I love Branson's smile. It's always been contagious, and I find myself smiling along with him even though he's being stingy with information.

"It's a surprise," he says, and I can tell he's not

willing to give me anything else.

"Okay, but is this, like, a *hang out in our PJs* kind of thing?"

"Well, I was thinking since you ditched me for winter formal—"

"You know that wasn't my fault!" I say, crushed he said that.

"I know," he says, "and if I recall, you already had a dress."

"I did. And it's so pretty." I hop off the bed to move toward my closet. "Do you wanna see it?"

He reaches out, grabs my arm, and stops me. "What I want is to see you wearing it tonight."

My eyes widen, as does my smile, and I sort of internally do a happy dance. I launch myself at him, pulling him up off the bed and into my arms, hugging him tightly.

"I take it that you like the idea?" he says when I finally let him go.

Our bodies stay pressed together as he slides his hands from my shoulders down the outside of my arms, where they eventually intertwine with mine.

I look up into his brown eyes. "I swear, you are so sweet. I'm so excited for you to see it. And I know it's not the same as being at school with all your friends, but—"

"I always have the best ideas," he says, repeating what I've told him numerous times over the years.

"Yes," I say, leaning in to give him a kiss on the cheek and wrapping my arms around his neck.

"What can I say?" he says. "Our friendship inspires me."

I happily kiss the side of his face again, but I'm already doing a mental countdown of how long I have to get ready. Because I got a little sweaty while playing soccer with Beck.

But then I think about what Branson said. About our *friendship*.

"And what do I do for you?" I breathe into his ear.

He swallows hard, and I wonder what he's thinking. "You make me happy, Laney. Seriously, I love to see you smile the way you just did when I told you to wear the dress."

Which is totally sweet. And had a slight romantic tone.

Okay, Lane. You have to stop dissecting everything he says.

Just put on your dress, go have fun, and see what—if anything—happens.

I hug him tightly again but notice that he backs away slightly.

Oh, that's not a good sign.

"Okay, so," he says, untangling himself from my arms, "I have to go home and get ready. See you soon."

And then he's gone.

I glance at the clock by my bed.

Crap! I only have forty-five minutes to get ready!

Thankfully, I washed my hair earlier today, but unfortunately, I then braided it when it was still wet. I undo it, expecting to see a frizzy disaster, but instead, I find really pretty waves that I think I can fix up in no time.

WHEN BRANSON SHOWS up at my house at seven, I'm not quite ready. Which ends up being okay because I enjoy making a slightly more dramatic entrance in my dress by floating down the stairs in it.

"This is for you," he says, handing me a wrist corsage.

Which I love.

My parents insist on taking a few photos of us, and then he takes me outside to Monroe's golf cart and over to the barn.

Once there, he leads me out to the new glass building, where all the party stuff from today is gone and a table for two sits in the center of the room. It's dark outside, and there are only a few candles burning around us, so we can see all the stars in the sky above it.

It's really pretty.

But then it starts snowing.

Inside.

Branson bows in front of me, takes my hand, and says, "May I have this dance?"

Music starts playing. A Christmas waltz.

We dance with the stars above us and the snow falling down on us.

And even though it's cold in here, I barely feel it.

Because I'm in Branson's arms.

And it's magical.

AFTER A FEW dances, I say, "This is really amazing,

Bran. How did you do all of it?"

"I had a little help."

"From who?"

"Christmas elves," he teases and then says, "Well, first, my dad, and then Mom overheard us and got involved."

"What did you tell them?"

"I told my dad that I wished we could have gone to formal together and asked him if he'd help me sort of re-create it. Like here. Like take you to dinner and go somewhere to dance. Of course, there are a lot of great restaurants in the area, but I couldn't find one that offered dancing too. He suggested the gazebo by the pond, but then Mom mentioned the snowmaker, which definitely fit the whole winter theme of the dance."

"What were the colors this year?"

"Blue and silver."

I look at the wrist corsage he gave me. And part of me feels like I could cry. I'm so touched. Because he did all this.

And as he holds me in his arms and gazes sweetly into my eyes, I tilt my chin upward in preparation for a kiss.

He shifts slightly, and it makes me wonder if he's nervous. Part of me feels like I should just kiss him already. Maybe that's what he wants—a *thank you* kiss. A *you're incredible* kiss.

But then his head drops a little lower, our noses touch, and his lips graze my cheek as he speaks. "You're my best friend, Laney. There isn't anything I wouldn't do for you."

And I know this is it. That perfect moment where our lips will come together, where soul will meet soul, where our breaths will collide—just like in the love poems I've read.

It's going to be the moment that changes things.

The moment of truth.

Will it be true love's kiss? Will the kiss overwhelm my senses and make me feel like he's the missing piece in the puzzle of my life?

I'm pretty sure I stop breathing in anticipation.

His lips leave my cheek when he leans back slightly and brings his hands up to gently cup my face. He gazes into my eyes and then kisses—my forehead.

And while it's the sweetest thing ever, I am so disappointed that I don't really notice him bending down until—*SPLAT!*

He launches cold, wet snow at me—waking me from my reverie and hitting me in the face like a slap of reality.

A *friendly* reality even though it felt like it had the potential to be so much more.

I decide not to dwell on all of it. Instead, I pick up some snow and toss it back at him.

Pretty soon, we're in a full-on snow war, running around like we did when we were kids.

Only I'm wearing a beautiful ballgown.

AFTER WE HAVE dinner, exchange gifts (he gave me a cute ladybug—or Laneybug—bracelet), and dance some more, he takes me home and tells me good night. And then I'm lying in bed as I think about what it must have looked like.

A scene out of one of my mom's romance movies. A pan shot from the outside of the glass conservatory, watching a snow fight between a beautiful boy in a tuxedo and a girl in a sparkling Tiffany Blue gown. It's the kind of scene that moviegoers would talk and dream about for years, hoping their Prince Charming would someday do something like that for them.

Although in the movie, it would go differently.

After the beautiful pan shot, the camera would move in closer as the boy hit the girl right in the face with the wet snow—which wouldn't ruin her makeup, like it did mine, or she possibly would just have a single mascara line down one cheek since she was laughing so hard during their fight that she was crying—and then the boy would move to wipe it from her beautiful glowing and slightly flushed face.

And there would be this moment between them.

The musical score would soar to a crescendo as their lips touched. But then the girl would shove snow down the boy's back with a laugh, which would only make him love her spunkiness more.

And *that's* when he'd sweep her into his arms and give her an epic movie-ending kiss.

Cut scene. Roll credits.

Hmm. Maybe I *am* a romantic at heart.

December 31st

ALL GROWN UP.
AUBREY LANE

I HELP ARDEN get ready for the party, curling her hair into ringlets and getting her into her dress—one that is a smaller version of mine. It's pink with a sparkly top and a full taffeta skirt.

"Let's go show Mom," I tell her, leading her down the stairs.

We find Mom's longtime stylist, Kym, in the kitchen.

"Well, don't you two look adorable," is what she says, but there's something in her tone that makes me feel like I'm in trouble. Especially when she says, "Come with me."

We go into Mom's dressing room, where she's sitting at her vanity, putting on makeup.

"Keatyn," Kym says, "I want you to take a photo of your two adorable little girls."

"Right now?" my mom asks, taken aback. It's obvious she's right in the middle of getting ready.

"Yes, *right now*," Kym states emphatically.

"Uh, okay," she says, grabbing her phone.

Arden and I have fun, posing together for some cute pictures.

"Wonderful," Kym says to us and then turns to Arden. "Why don't you show your dad your pretty dress? He's in the den."

"Yay!" she yells out, doing a little twirl in the middle of the room before rushing off.

ONCE SHE'S GONE, Kym lets out a big sigh and looks at my mother. "Keatyn, seriously? Lane cannot wear this dress. She looks twelve. Make that eight. Matching dresses? And a braid? Really?"

I look down at my dress. I mean, it's not nearly as slinky as the stretchy gold lamé one that's clinging to my mom's body in all the right places, but the skirt is fun to twirl around in.

My mom opens her mouth to say something, but Kym continues, "She's fifteen. She's not your little girl anymore."

Mom studies me with a shrewd eye and then sighs. "I suppose you're right."

"But you picked this dress out, Mom."

"Yeah, well," Kym says, "you should see what *she* used to wear to the club when she was your age."

"She went to clubs at my age?" Literally, I'm shocked.

"She did," Kym says with a smirk toward Mom. "But luckily for you, I anticipated this and brought you a dress of my own design. Made just for you."

"Really?" I throw my arms around her. "Oh, Miss Kym, thank you so much."

"You haven't even seen the dress yet," Kym counters.

"It was really thoughtful, regardless."

"You are so very polite," Kym says to me, but she's eyeing my mother as she hands me a dress bag. "Why don't you go put it on and then come back out and surprise us?"

I head to my mom's huge walk-in closet and let my eyes survey the rows of designer dresses, handbags, and shoes. When she's at home, she always looks nice, but she's never all decked out like she is for publicity events or when filming. I mean, we live on a vineyard. It's a working farm, where we harvest grapes and olives and also grow the majority of the fruits and vegetables that we eat.

Most of what I wear around is practical for the setting—jeans and boots. Sure, I have swimsuits for when we go on vacation to the beach and stuff like that, but clothes have never really been a big deal for me.

But when I interned in Paris last summer, my dad took me shopping to some really pretty stores and made me get what he said were appropriate clothes for his intern daughter. It consisted of mostly blazers, skirts, dress pants, and ballet flats that I left at our house there. I mean, it's not like I'd wear them around here.

This section of my mom's closet is full of sparkle. Lots of pinks, golds, and sequins. And all really beautiful.

I glance at what I'm wearing again. I look pretty in it. The pink flatters my skin.

But then I think about the knit dress I wore for Christmas Eve and how much Branson liked it. Maybe Kym's right. Maybe I don't want to be in a dress that matches my little sister.

Maybe this new dress will make Branson realize he loves me. Realize he desperately needs to kiss me.

I unzip the garment bag she gave me to find a really pretty dress. When I put it on, I like it even better. It's black with a halter-style neckline, and the top and empire waist are trimmed in oversize pearls. The skirt is short and flirty, but it's actually a skort, meaning I won't have to worry about my underwear showing when I dance.

At the bottom of the bag is a shoebox with a pair of boots—*designer* boots. Even though us kids aren't allowed social media accounts, it doesn't mean I'm not aware of all the beautiful designer clothing that people send to my mom. Or that I don't read fashion magazines. And these boots are supposedly a very big trend this year—black patent ankle boots with oversize pearls on a strap around the top. But there are more reasons besides their label to love them. First, they only have a little heel and will be comfortable, and second, they give the dress an edgier vibe than, say, a classic pump would.

I go back out to show them, and I know that I must be beaming. I like the way I look, but I'm afraid my mom will say the dress is too short and make me put the other dress back on. It's funny really. I was fine with that dress until I put this one on. Now, I never want to take this one off.

"What do you think?"

"It's adorable," my mom says, which causes me to smile bigger. "And still age-appropriate."

"Of course it is," Kym teases. "I can't believe you would doubt me after all these years."

My mom isn't big on me wearing much makeup.

She says I don't need it. That I have naturally beautiful skin. But I look at Kym's long eyelashes and thick eyeliner and figure I might as well go for it.

"Kym, would you help me do my hair and makeup to match?"

"I'd be honored," she says.

I DON'T GET false lashes, but with shimmering gold eye shadow smudged on my lids and under my eye, liquid black liner swooped on the lash line, and three coats of mascara, I don't really need them. My green eyes look huge. Kym adds a little nude lip stain, and I'm ready for the party.

The outside of our home is still lit with white Christmas lights, and there are even lights on some of the rows of grapes in the field beyond. There's a lot of commotion going on in the barn, so I take a peek inside, finding that my cousins—Jagger, Jett, and Cash Moran—are onstage, doing a sound check. Their dad, Damian, is a record producer and former lead singer of a band called Twisted Dreams, and he's married to my dad's sister, Peyton. My cousins have their own band and will be taking the stage along with other musicians and a celebrity DJ tonight.

"Lane!" Cash calls out, jumping off the stage and giving me a hug.

He's only a year older than me, and we've always been close.

"Are you guys going to play anything new to-night?" I ask him.

"Speaking of new," he says, "look at you."

"Are you sure I don't look weird? I don't normally wear this much makeup."

"You look really nice," he says sweetly. "You might have to be in our next music video."

"Really? That would be kind of fun."

He looks around to see if anyone is listening to us and says, "Wanna know a secret?"

"Of course I do."

"I saw one of my dad's old videos from when Twisted Dreams was first getting famous, and your mom was in it. And get this, she was wearing a bikini."

"Ew. Really? Which song?"

"It was 'Meet Me at the Beach.' I've always liked that one."

"Ah, me too. It's one of my favorite oldies."

"My point is, your parents couldn't say no."

"Ha! True! Although I don't know what I would do in it."

"Dance, maybe?"

"Well, that is one thing I am good at. Did you have a good Christmas in St. Croix?"

"Yeah, it was great. Got a little too much sun the first day. Drank one too many rum punches the second. Surfed. Ate. It was all good. Oh, and the best part, we got some good news."

"What kind of news?"

"You know how we put a bunch of our music up on that streaming service for free, just to get people used to our sound?"

"Yeah."

"They asked for more. Apparently, we're trending. I mean, we already have an album, but we could get offered a touring gig because of this."

"That would be so cool, Cash." I give him another hug. "You know I love your music."

He lowers his voice. "Dad's never been a country

music fan, so I'm not sure he gets our vibe of mixing it with a little rapping, but we love it and hope big things are to come. And I think he's starting to see the potential."

"That's a good thing," I tell him, before going up onstage to give my other cousins and Uncle Damian a hug.

I'm just stepping off the stage when Aunt Peyton grabs me, spins me around to face her, and looks at me with wide eyes. "Lane!"

"Aunt Peyton!" I say in reply.

"You look adorable! All grown up."

My mouth forms a broad grin because I hope that someone in particular thinks that I look grown up enough to kiss tonight.

HAPPILY EVER AFTER.
KEATYN

"YOU'VE OUTDONE YOURSELF," I say to Ariela as we enter the party barn.

Winter wonderland is gone and replaced with a ceiling of gold twinkle lights, gold disco balls, and lots of navy velvet. It's shimmering and sophisticated.

"Thank you. We're doing a *Kiss Me at Midnight* theme, thus the midnight-blue color. We've sectioned off some seating areas with drapery, so you will be able to sit and chat or relax, even with the music thumping around you. Heavy appetizers. A champagne fountain," she says as she walks me through the areas that are already starting to fill up with family and friends. "But I have to say, the most fun I had was coming up with something to do with the glass structure. Which, honestly, sort of led to the whole theme."

"Oh my gosh!" I say because I am floored by what I see in front of me.

She added pieces to the outside of the glass structure and somehow made it look like a big fairy-tale coach. Gold wheels sit on the corners of the building, and a painting between the wheels makes it look like the building is suspended over a road. There are golden scrolls that attach the building to bigger-than-life horses, and instead of entering on the ground level, she added gold stairs and apparently took a large window out of the structure and made it into a door.

She grabs my hand and pulls me up the stairs. I expect to go back down a set of stairs to the ground level, but she's built a new floor up on a platform, so you literally step right in. The ceiling is draped with gold lamé and more navy velvet along with gold twinkle lights. Velvet cushioned seats are set in rows. And at the front, I notice a little stage area with what appears to be a wedding arch.

As soon as my eyes go to the arch, she does a little happy jump. "It's a surprise, but Riley and I are going to renew our vows tonight, like in the middle of the party. So, I might have gone a little overboard."

I reach out and give my friend a hug. She's made Riley so happy since she came back into his life. They have three adorable children—a son, Mason, who is fourteen, and then they bucked the Johnson family tradition of boys and managed to have two girls—Emerson, who is thirteen, and baby Addison, who is a year and a half.

"I'm so happy for you," I tell her.

"And happy for me," Riley says as he puts his arms around both of our shoulders.

"I'm happy for you because you were smart enough to marry this one."

"And I counter that I tried to marry her when we were eighteen. I always knew she was the one."

To which, honestly, neither Ariela or I have a comeback for. He has always loved her.

"True," I finally say.

"What do you think?" Ariela asks Riley.

He pulls her into his arms and gives her a kiss. "Your wedding planning skills have come up a notch or two since our first New Year's Eve wedding. Really, this is incredible. Like a fairy tale."

She grins at him. "Actually, it's the continuation of our happily ever after."

He grins back. "That's what I told you when I asked you to marry me, didn't I?"

"You sure did."

AFTER ARIELA FLITS away—going to check in with her long-time assistant, Kyle, to make sure everything is how it should be—Riley stands next to me and grins. "I know what you're thinking."

"What?" I say, trying to pretend I don't know what he's talking about. We shouldn't be talking shop tonight.

"We *have* to work this gorgeous setup into our next project."

"I couldn't agree more," I say.

ALMOST MIDNIGHT.
AUBREY LANE

THE PARTY IS in full swing before I find Branson.

"I have good news!" I tell him.

"Your parents are letting you come to Eastbrooke in January?"

"Oh, no. But you know how I did that internship for a few weeks in Paris last summer? My mom told me that this year, they are letting me go to London! For the whole summer!"

"Why would you do that?" he says, looking mad. "We could have spent all summer together."

"Oh, I'm still planning on going to the Hamptons for the summer kickoff. I'll go to London from there. It's a big deal for me and I'm super excited."

"Whatever," he says and then walks away before I even get the chance to tell him that I want him to come with me. That my parents are okay with it if his are.

But as I am following him through the crowd, Beck grabs me. "There you are!" He stands in front of me and goes, "You look . . . wow."

"Wow?" I say, narrowing my eyes at him.

"Yeah, wow."

"Um, good wow or, like, *wow, I can't believe she wore that* wow?"

He sets one hand onto my hip and moves closer to me as a smile breaks out on his face. "It's a surprised wow. A *where's the braid and cowboy boots* wow." His other hand slides under my hair, finding the back of my neck as he murmurs, "I've been dying to kiss you."

His lips quickly press against mine, soft and warm,

and are gone before I realize what happened.

I just had my first kiss.

And although I thought it might be fun to kiss Beck when we were playing soccer, I was still holding out hope that my first kiss would be with Branson.

I look around us to see if Branson saw.

I'm confused, and I don't know what to think.

Because even though Beck's not the guy I wished for, the kiss, while quick, was actually kinda nice.

Maybe the shooting star knew that Branson and I weren't meant to be.

And it's hard to argue with a shooting star.

Especially when Beck spins me out in a dance move and then draws me back in, causing us to crash into each other.

He takes a step back and gives me a once-over, and then he pulls on my long curls. "I kinda miss the braid, but you look really pretty tonight, Lane."

"Thank you," I say, feeling a little embarrassed by his compliment at the same time my heart starts soaring.

"I heard there are carriage rides out front. What do you say?" he asks, nodding toward the door.

And all of a sudden, I feel bold, so I place my hand in his and say, "Only if you promise to kiss me again."

He chuckles. "I think I can manage that."

THE CARRIAGE RIDE is, in one word, amazing.

Beck looks exceptionally hot tonight. All the Johnson boys are cute, but Beck by far has the best hair of all the cousins. Even when everyone else's is windblown or messy at the beach, his is always perfectly in place. Like it doesn't know how to lie any other way. The only deviation from the perfection is a little cowlick in the front that makes it stick up over his right eye, but that only adds to the appeal.

We are wrapped together in a blanket, and my legs are crossed on top of his.

And he's kissing me.

The kisses started out sweet, like the first one, but has progressed to more. So, not only is this the night of my first real kiss, but it's also my first make-out session. And I'm loving the way it feels.

I mean, there hasn't actually been tongues involved yet, but I think there might be.

Depending on how long he keeps telling the driver to *take another lap.*

At some point, he wraps his arm around my shoulders, allowing me to lean back and look up at the brilliant stars dotting the sky.

I let out a little sigh and thank the stars for tonight—although I still don't understand why Branson just got mad and walked away from me.

But I'm not going to even think about it.

I'm here. With Beck.

And I'm having fun.

EVENTUALLY, WE RETURN to the party.

Beck glances at his watch. "Our timing is *literally* perfect. It's almost midnight. I'm going to run grab us some champagne. Meet me out in the middle of the dance floor."

I do as he asked, finding a spot just as the countdown starts.

"*Ten. Nine. Eight. Seven. Six. Five. Four. Three.*

Two. One," is shouted out by the crowd.

I feel a tap on my shoulder and turn around, where I find Branson.

And maybe it is the combined magic of the power of the shooting star mixed with the significance of the timing, but it feels like time is standing still.

I barely hear the party noise going on around us.

All my nerve endings seem to have been relocated to just the two spots on my body that are touching his. His hands in mine.

"Happy New Year, Laneybug," he says, his gaze demanding my full attention.

But then he leans in and kisses me.

His lips are soft and plump, but are pressing firmly against mine in a possessiveness I've never felt from him before.

And maybe it's because it's midnight at the start of a new year, but it's like his lips are branding mine, tattooing his name across them so that everyone will know that I'm his for the year.

And even though my eyes are closed, it's like the sky is lit up with a thousand shooting stars.

"That was an amazing first kiss," he says tenderly, leaning his forehead against mine.

"It was," I agree. And I'm not lying. It *was* the first kiss of my dreams.

Except that is wasn't *actually* my first kiss.

But I guess it was ours.

And that's all the matters.

"I told you I'd kiss you at midnight," he says with a grin. "And you know what that means."

"That I'll be yours all year?"

"Yes, I've wanted to kiss you since I got back home—well, since like forever, really—and it's been so hard waiting. But I wanted your first kiss—*our* first kiss—to be really special. Sorry I got mad and stormed off earlier. I looked all over and couldn't find you. But when the countdown started, there you were, waiting in the middle of the dance floor for me, just like a dream."

My heart feels like it drops out of my chest, and I know that I need to tell him where I was. And that it wasn't actually my first kiss.

But he goes, "I'll go grab us some punch. Wait here."

NEXT THING I know, Beck is at my side, handing me a flute of champagne.

"Better late than never. Happy New Year, Lane," he says, clinking his glass against mine and then downing the champagne in one long gulp.

"Happy New Year," I mumble, but I can't stop thinking about my kiss with Branson.

About what it means.

Does the fact that we kissed at midnight mean I'll be his all year?

Or will the fact that I kissed Beck ruin our chance?

And what will happen when I go to Eastbrooke with both of them this fall?

Get ready for the next generation at Eastbrooke!
Best Friends Aren't Forever
Eastbrooke Academy – Book One

About the Author

Jillian Dodd® is a *USA Today* and Amazon Top 10 best-selling author. She writes fun binge-able romance series with characters her readers fall in love with—from the boy next door in the That Boy series to the daughter of a famous actress in The Keatyn Chronicles® to a spy who might save the world in the Spy Girl® series. Her newest series include London Prep, a prep school series about a drama filled three-week exchange, and the Sex in the City-ish chick lit series, Kitty Valentine.

Jillian is married to her college sweetheart, adores writing big fat happily ever afters, wears a lot of pink, buys way too many shoes, loves to travel, and is distracted by anything covered in glitter.

Made in the USA
Middletown, DE
10 January 2022